MW01690448

This book belongs to:

the Bride

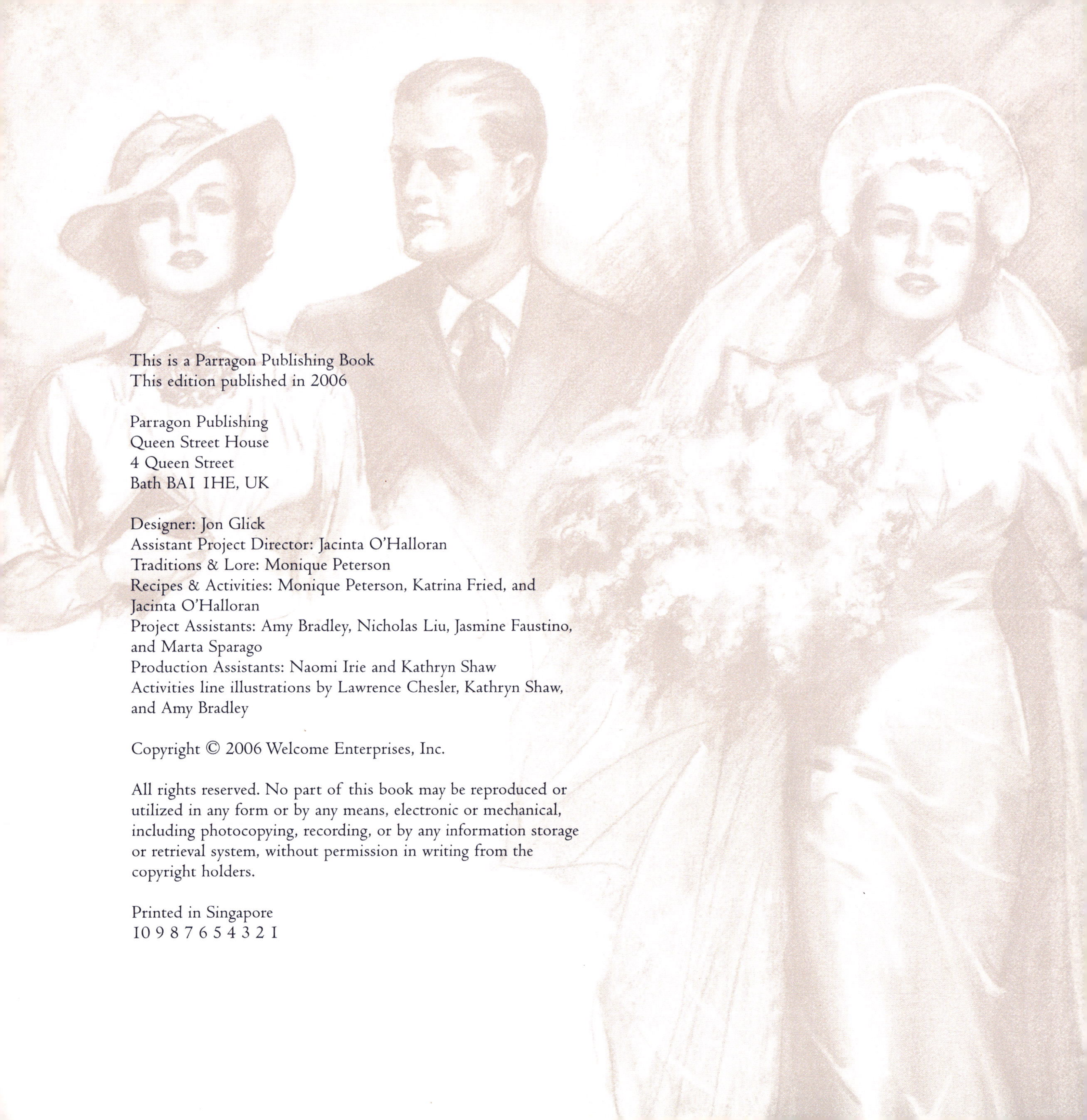

This is a Parragon Publishing Book
This edition published in 2006

Parragon Publishing
Queen Street House
4 Queen Street
Bath BA1 1HE, UK

Designer: Jon Glick
Assistant Project Director: Jacinta O'Halloran
Traditions & Lore: Monique Peterson
Recipes & Activities: Monique Peterson, Katrina Fried, and Jacinta O'Halloran
Project Assistants: Amy Bradley, Nicholas Liu, Jasmine Faustino, and Marta Sparago
Production Assistants: Naomi Irie and Kathryn Shaw
Activities line illustrations by Lawrence Chesler, Kathryn Shaw, and Amy Bradley

Copyright © 2006 Welcome Enterprises, Inc.

All rights reserved. No part of this book may be reproduced or utilized in any form or by any means, electronic or mechanical, including photocopying, recording, or by any information storage or retrieval system, without permission in writing from the copyright holders.

Printed in Singapore
10 9 8 7 6 5 4 3 2 1

The secret of a happy marriage remains a secret.

HENNY YOUNGMAN

Table of Contents

LITERARY EXCERPTS

ESSAYS & NON-FICTION

TRADITIONS & LORE

POETRY

ACTIVITIES

RECIPES

Unwed women have long relied on love charms and divinations to foretell the meeting of future husbands and ensure marital happiness. You may already be on your way to the altar, but it can't hurt to make sure Fate agrees with your choice. Here are a few ways women have quelled their curiosity about the men of their dreams:

He loves me, he loves me not . . .

- ON CHRISTMAS EVE, stand before the fireplace and gaze into the flames to see the image of your future husband.

- IF YOU LOVE A MAN and want to know if he will propose, throw a nut into the fire and say his name. If the nut jumps, you'll marry. If the nut doesn't move, the relationship will have no spark.

In case you are lucky enough to be a bridesmaid, plant a sprig of myrtle in front of the newlyweds' home. If it takes root, you'll marry within the year.

You can learn the temperament of your future husband by plucking a piece of hay from a hayloft at midnight. A crooked piece foretells a surly man; a straight piece signifies a good-natured mate.

❦ PEEL AN APPLE in a single strip and toss the peel over your left shoulder. The shape of the peel will reveal the first letter of the name of your spouse to be.

❦ Or pluck some wild daisies from a nearby field and put the roots under your pillow to dream of your groom.

❦ On All Hallows Eve, brush your hair three times in front of a mirror. If you glimpse a man standing behind you, wedding bells will ring before the year is through.

❦ When attending a wedding, be sure to take a piece of groom's cake home and put it under your pillow. That night the face of your future husband will appear in your dreams.

❦ If that doesn't work, soak your shoelaces in water until they're saturated. Then throw them against the wall to see the initials of your soon-to-be betrothed.

I will tell you the real secret of how to stay married. Keep the cave clean. They want the cave clean and spotless. Air-conditioned, if possible. Sharpen his spear, and stick it in his hand when he goes out in the morning to spear that bear; and when the bear chases him, console him when he comes home at night, and tell him what a big man he is, and then hide the spear so he doesn't fall over it and stab himself…

JEROME CHODOROV AND JOSEPH FIELDS

If ever two were one, then surely we.
If ever man were loved by wife, then thee;
If ever wife was happy in a man,
Compare with me ye women if you can.
I prize thy love more than whole mines of gold,
Or all the riches that the East doth hold.
My love is such that rivers cannot quench,
Nor ought but love from thee, give recompence.
Thy love is such I can no way repay,
The heavens reward thee manifold I pray.
Then while we live, in love lets so persevere,
That when we live no more, we may live ever.

TO MY DEAR AND LOVING HUSBAND
Anne Bradstreet

For ages people who've hardly known each other, let alone come to love each other, have united through the divine wisdom of match-makers and fortune-tellers. Such bonds cement families, strengthen clans, and in the case of royal marriages, seal political contracts. If a good match can be foretold in the stars, all the better.

A match made in heaven

ACCORDING TO CHINESE LORE, the gods unite each couple at birth with an invisible red cord. In time, the cord grows shorter, drawing the pair together. The pivotal role of the matchmaker is to help these predestined people find each other, according to the 3,000-year-old practice of astrology. The matchmaker evaluates a possible union on the principals of the Eight Characters or Four Pillars. She writes down characters identifying the birth hour, day, month, and year of the prospective bride and groom on rice paper. According to some practices, if the characters are lucky and if nothing bad happens in three days, the marriage can be considered a good match.

When the time comes, the matchmaker hosts a betrothal tea for the groom and his parents. The prospective bride serves the tea. If the groom wishes to pursue marriage, he will place an embroidered red satchel on his saucer. The bride may accept his offer by taking the bag. If she is not interested, she will have politely left the room before the groom has an opportunity to show his interest.

A family starts with a young man falling in love with a girl. No superior alternative has been found.

WINSTON CHURCHILL

November 29, 1866

My Dear Miss,

I now take up my pen to write to you hoping these few lines will find you well as it leaves me at present Thank God for it. You will perhaps be surprised that I should make so bold as to write to you who is such a lady and I hope you will not be vex at me for it. I hardly dare say what I want, I am so timid about ladies, and my heart trimmels like a hespin. But I once seed in a book that faint heart never won fair lady, so here goes.

HOPEFUL PROPOSAL TO A YOUNG LADY OF THE VILLAGE

A REAL PROPOSAL LETTER

BY SIMON FALLOWFIELD

I am a farmer in a small way and my age is rather more than forty years and my mother lives with me and keeps my house, and she has been very poorly lately and cannot stir about much and I think I should be more comfortabler with a wife.

I have had my eye on you a long time and I think you are a very nice young woman and one that would make me happy if only you think so. We keep a servant girl to milk three kye and do the work in the house, and she goes on a bit in the summer to gadder wickens and she snags a few of turnips in the back kend. I do a piece of work on the farm myself and attends Pately Market, and I sometimes show a few sheep and I feeds between 3 & 4 pigs agen Christmas, and the same is very useful in the house to make pies and cakes and so forth, and I sells the hams to help pay for the barley meal.

I have about 73 pund in Naisbro Bank and we have a nice little parlour downstairs with a blue carpet, and an oven on the side of the fireplace and the old woman on the other side smoking. The Golden Rules claimed up on the walls above the long settle, and you could sit all day in the easy chair and knit and mend my kytles and leggums, and you could make the tea ready agin I come in, and you could make butter for Pately Market, and I would drive you to church every Sunday in the spring cart, and I would do all that bees in my power to make you happy. So I hope to hear from you. I am in desprit and Yurnest, and will marry you at May Day, or if my mother dies afore I shall want you afore. If only you will accept of me, my dear, we could be very happy together.

I hope you will let me know your mind by return of post, and if you are favourable I will come up to scratch. So no more at present from your well-wisher and true love—

Simon Fallowfield

P.S. I hope you will say nothing about this. If you will not accept of me I have another very nice woman in my eye, and I think I shall marry her if you do not accept of me, but I thought you would suit me mother better, she being very crusty at times. So I tell you now before you come, she will be Maister.

THIS PROPOSAL WAS REFUSED BY MARY FOSTER,
THE LOCAL BEAUTY OF MIDDLEMOOR, PATELY BRIDGE, IN YORKSHIRE.

My most brilliant achievement was my ability to be able to persuade my wife to marry me.

WINSTON CHURCHILL

Say you'll be mine

A candlelight dinner for two; a walk in the park hand in hand; a delivery of long-stemmed red roses. Ah, sweet romance! Dating customs of love-smitten men have ranged from the boisterous to the sublime—and have been, in some cases, less than virtuous! While your wedding may signify the end of courtship, it certainly does not mean the death of romance. Find inspiration in the following wooing traditions and keep your marriage full of passion.

THE ART OF SHOWERING one's true love with poems and serenades did not fade with Romeo and Juliet. Affection-seeking gentlemen in Spain, Brazil, and the Philippines still take this tradition very seriously. They hope to win the hearts of their beloved with verses they've composed themselves. Often they'll invite a group of friends to accompany them with musical instruments while they sing and dance until the wee hours of the morning.

IN MID-TWENTIETH-CENTURY AMERICA, the custom of dating involved time spent together on the porch swing or going to a drive-in movie. But during colonial times, couples courted between the sheets! English and Dutch emigrants from rural communities introduced this custom, called bundling, which was touted as a way to save on heating costs. Families permitted wooing couples to get to know each other—fully or partially dressed—in bed. A "bundling board" placed in the bed was supposed to separate the lovebirds and keep them chaste. Preventive measures weren't always failsafe, however, resulting in more than one pregnant bride at the altar....

HOW DOES A WOMAN SHOW that her heart belongs to someone? By spooning with her sweetheart, of course. What has come to be known as necking or snuggling got its start from an old Welsh custom. A man would woo his beloved with an elaborately carved wooden spoon. If she accepted his affections, she would attach it to a ribbon and wear it around her neck as a sign of betrothal.

IN RURAL POLAND, a man might show his feelings for a woman by visiting her and inquiring about purchasing a horse. If, during their conversation, he reveals a bottle of vodka wrapped in red ribbons and flowers, she'll know the visit has nothing to do with her horse. Instead of asking for her hand in marriage, he'll simply ask for a glass. If she is ready to be his bride, she'll return with glasses and her family to celebrate their betrothal.

IN MANY AFRICAN VILLAGES, courtship is not between two people, but between two families. If a prospective suitor wishes to inquire about a certain unwed female, he might send his mother, aunt, or other married female relative to knock on her family's door. She asks to arrange a meeting of family members and village elders. The prospective suitor will bring gifts of money, grain, produce, and livestock to show his ability to provide for his new bride and future family.

War of the Posies

In England, suitors were mad about flowers, especially during Victorian times, when virtually everything that bloomed carried a special symbolism. When a young man wished to gain the affection of a certain young woman, he would send her posies that held secret messages. She would reply in kind with specific flowers that would either welcome or shun his attentions. Here's a sampling of petal lore:

Ambrosia— "Love returned"
Burdock— "Touch me not"
Camellia— "You are perfected loveliness"
Currant— "Thy frown will kill me"
Daffodil— "Unrequited love"
Narcissus— "Uncertainty"
Pansies— "Think of me"
Peach blossoms— "Am I your captive?"
Pink rose— "Our love is perfect happiness"
Ranunculus— "You are radiant with charm"
Red columbine— "Anxious and trembling"
Wild daisy— "I will think of it"

I go about murmuring, 'I have made that dignified girl commit herself, I have, I have,' and then I vault over the sofa with exultation.

WALTER BAGEHOT

(MARRIED HIS LOVE ELIZABETH WILSON IN 1858)

Do you  all for me,

and my Love is as soft

as an  For you

 Hair and 

of my eye, so if we 

anyhow, for I know we w

for my heart  for you

as a  but as strong

are a 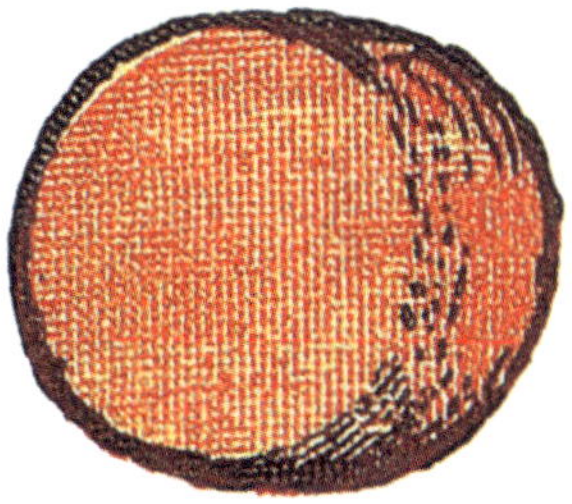 with your

nose. You are the 

then  marry,

uld make a happy 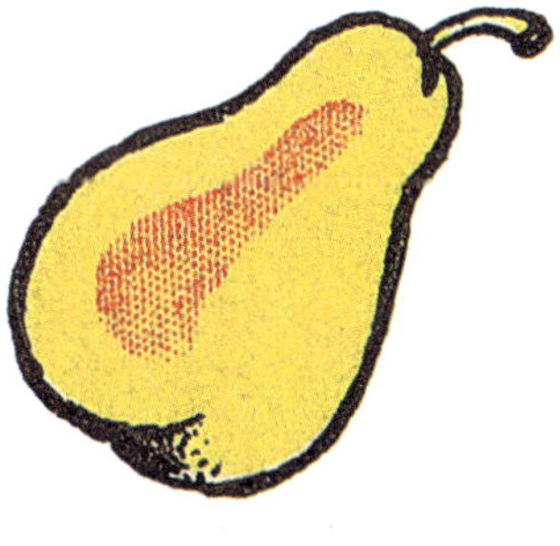

Come live with me and be my love,
And we will all the pleasures prove
That hills and valleys, dales and fields
And all the craggy mountains yields.

There we will sit upon the rocks
And see the shepherds feed their flocks,
By shallow rivers to whose falls
Melodious birds sing madrigals.

And I will make thee beds of roses
With a thousand fragrant posies,
A cap of flowers and a kirtle
Embroidered all with leaves of myrtle.

A gown made of the finest wool
Which from our pretty lambs we pull;
Fair lined slippers for the cold,
With buckles of the purest gold;

A belt of straw and ivy buds,
With coral clasps and amber studs:
And if these pleasures may thee move,
Come live with me and be my love.

The shepherds' swains shall dance
and sing
For thy delight each May morning:
If these delights thy mind may move,
Then live with me and be my love.

THE PASSIONATE SHEPHERD
TO HIS LOVE
Christopher Marlowe

You're engaged! It's unmistakable: Friends and strangers alike know it's official when they see an engagement ring on your finger. But how did the ring become a symbol of marital unity?

This ring is round and hath no end

In ancient Rome, husbands promised commitment to their wives with rings made of iron. Those too poor to afford a ring would seal their engagement with the loop of a door key to the new marital home. Some of the earliest rings were not metal at all, but made of woven grasses or leather. Others were carved out of ivory or bone. In A.D. 860, Pope Nicholas I decreed a new mandate for the Catholic world to ensure that engagements would be binding: From then on, the ring was not only a requirement for nuptial intent but should be made of a valuable metal, preferably gold.

Ancient Egyptians believed the ring, a perfect circle, represented a supernatural link to eternal love shared by two people. This is just one of the many shades of cultural meaning that rings have had throughout the history of marriage.

So is my love unto my friend

Throughout medieval times, the betrothal ring was also used as a wedding ring. It is not until the fifteenth century that both a betrothal and wedding ring were given. Historically, men have chosen not to wear wedding rings; it was not until the popularity of the gimmal ring in the sixteenth century that they began to embrace the idea. Double-ring ceremonies became fashionable in the United States during World War II, as the ring became a tangible link to home for young husbands posted overseas. The custom has endured to the present.

ELIZABETHANS WORE the double- or triple-banded gimmal ring, so named for the Latin word *geminius*, which means "twin." Traditionally, the engaged woman wore one band and her groom-to-be wore the second. If the ring contained a third band, a witness to the engagement wore it as additional proof of the couple's betrothal. On the wedding day, all the bands would be reunited on the bride's ring finger.

RENOWNED FOR THEIR LOVE of poetry and flowers, the Elizabethans exchanged poesy rings with mottoes or poetic love couplets known as poesies engraved on the inside or outside of the band.

USUALLY HANDED DOWN from mother to daughter in Ireland, the Claddagh ring features two hands holding a crowned heart. The crown is worn so that it points toward the wrist on betrothal; upon marriage, the wearer turns the ring around so that the crown faces outward.

THE CELTIC LOVE-KNOT RING, a symbol of eternity, unity, and fidelity, is made of intertwined, unending lines.

IN COLONIAL AMERICA, a young man would give his beloved a wedding thimble upon betrothal. On the wedding day, the bride would cut off the bottom of the thimble and wear it as her wedding ring.

IN FRANCE, it is customary to engrave the bride's name and half of the wedding date on one wedding band and the groom's name and the other half of the date on the other ring. The names and wedding date then come together as the rings are slipped onto the finger during the ceremony.

IN THE 1870S, Tiffany & Co. designed the first ring with the tone set above the band. This famous Tiffany setting has come to epitomize the modern engagement ring.

AN OLD IRISH TRADITION had the man presenting his intended with a woven bracelet of human hair as a symbol of his unending love.

VICTORIANS LOVED to spell messages with gemstones in their rings. For example, **R**uby, **E**merald, **G**arnet, **A**methyst, **R**uby, **D**iamond says "regard," while **L**apis lazuli, **O**pal, **V**erde antique, **E**merald spells "love."

For years my wedding ring has done its job. It has led me not into temptation. It has reminded my husband numerous times at parties that it's time to go home. It has been a source of relief to a dinner companion. It has been a status symbol in the maternity ward.

ERMA BOMBECK

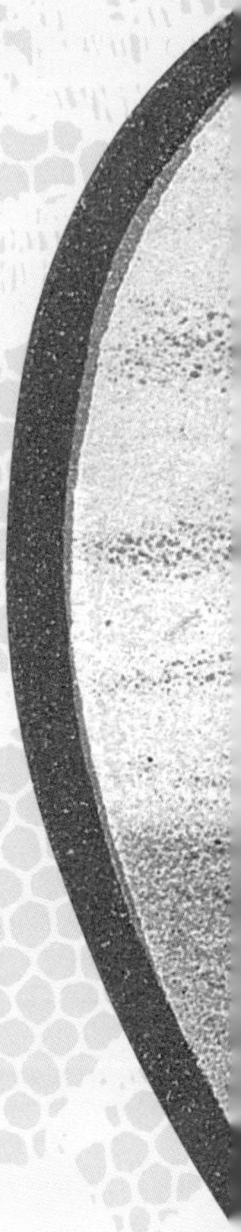

Julia, I bring
To thee this ring,
Made for thy finger fit;
To show by this
That our love is
Or should be, like to it.

Loose though it be,
The joint is free;
So, when love's yoke is on,
It must not gall,
Nor fret at all,
With hard oppression.

But it must play,
Still either way,
And be, too, such a yoke
As not too wide
To overslide,
Or be so straight to choke.

So we who bear
This beam, must rear
Ourselves to such a height
As that the stay
Of either may
Create the burthen light.

And as this round
Is nowhere found
To flaw, or else to sever,
So let our love
As endless prove,
And pure as gold forever.

TO JULIA
Robert Herrick

Diamonds are a girl's best friend

What's in a stone? Fortune or misfortune, depending on whom you ask. The "true blue" SAPPHIRE promises marital happiness. But the unlucky EMERALD spells jealousy for its wearer, unless the bride-to-be is Irish or born in May, in which case emeralds are highly lucky and will strengthen the eyes, too. Many women have shunned PEARLS because they look like oyster's tears and are feared to bring on a weepy marriage. But Asian brides know that pearls not only stop newlywed tears, but also promote good health and marital bliss. Only October-born brides should wear OPALS, otherwise their changing colors foretell a distrustful marriage. The DIAMOND, perhaps the world's most popular engagement gemstone, is quite lucky. Light that reflects off the brilliant stone wards off jealous evil spirits. For those interested in becoming parents, wearing a diamond will encourage fertility, especially if it touches the skin. Furthermore, wearing a rock that symbolizes eternal and singular love is sure to soothe marital arguments. But the bride who wears an engagement ring with her birthstone may be the luckiest of all.

MONTH	STONE	SYMBOLISM
JANUARY	GARNET	CONSTANCY, FIDELITY
FEBRUARY	AMETHYST	SINCERITY
MARCH	AQUAMARINE	COURAGE
APRIL	DIAMOND	INNOCENCE, PURITY
MAY	EMERALD	HAPPINESS, SUCCESS IN LOVE
JUNE	PEARL	BEAUTY
JULY	RUBY	LOVE, CLARITY OF HEART
AUGUST	PERIDOT	JOY
SEPTEMBER	SAPPHIRE	WISDOM, FAITHFULNESS
OCTOBER	OPAL	CONSISTENCY, FEARLESSNESS
NOVEMBER	TOPAZ	FIDELITY
DECEMBER	TURQUOISE	SUCCESS, PROSPERITY

ENGAGEMENT COCKTAIL PARTY

Often hosted by the bride and groom or their families, a stylish and love-themed cocktail soirée is a simple yet elegant way to celebrate your engagement. Our recipes for champagne punch and delicious heart shaped hors d'oeuvres are the perfect accompaniments for a night of romance. Just add a little Sinatra in the background, tons of candles, some gorgeous flowers and enjoy the moment.

CHAMPAGNE PUNCH

1/2 cup sugar
1 pineapple, chopped
1 cup fresh lemon juice
1 cup fresh orange juice
2 cups light rum
2/3 cup Cointreau
2/3 cup grenadine
2 bottles champagne, chilled
2 cups ice
Mint leaves and thin orange slices for garnish

1. Combine sugar and pineapple in a large punch bowl. Set aside for 1 hour.
2. Add lemon juice, orange juice, rum, Cointreau and grenadine. Chill for 2 hours.
3. Right before serving add champagne and ice. Garnish each glass with orange slice and mint sprig.

Serves 8-10

LOVELY HORS D'OEUVRES

Delicious and delightful, these sweet heart shaped finger sandwiches are the perfect accompaniment to the Champagne punch. For the toast, we recommend using a loaf of Italian bread (Ciabatta is good) from any gourmet deli, though regular sandwich bread will work, as well. Prepare bite-sized toasts as instructed below and serve with any one of our suggested toppings, or use a favorite recipe of your own.

MINI HEART SHAPED TOASTS

3 loaves white bread
extra virgin olive oil
small heart shaped cookie cutter

Thinly slice the bread and cut out heart shapes with the cookie cutter. Arrange the individual hearts on a baking sheet, drizzle with olive oil, and toast until golden brown. Toasts may be made up to one day in advance and stored in an airtight container at room temperature.

Makes approximately 120 small heart shaped toasts. (Quantity will vary depending on size of cookie cutter and bread loaf.)

CAVIAR TOPPING

6 tablespoons crème fraiche
2 ounces high quality caviar

Thinly spread crème fraiche on heart toasts and top with a small dollop of caviar. Keep covered until ready to serve.

Makes approximately 40 Caviar Toasts.

CHOPPED TOMATO AND PARMESAN TOPPING

4 large tomatoes, chopped
1 red onion, chopped
4 tablespoons olive oil
2 teaspoon fresh basil, finely chopped
4 teaspoons fresh parsley, finely chopped
½ cup freshly grated Parmesan cheese
salt and pepper to taste

1. In a large bowl, combine tomatoes, onion, olive oil, basil, parsley, salt and pepper.
2. Place heart toasts on baking sheet and top with tomato mixture. Sprinkle with Parmesan cheese.
3. Broil for 2-3 minutes or until Parmesan cheese has completely melted. Cool for 3-5 minutes and serve warm.

Makes approximately 40 Tomato and Parmesan Toasts.

MUSHROOM AND GOAT'S CHEESE TOPPING

10 medium sized field mushrooms, sliced
4 tablespoons butter
1 red chili, finely diced
2 shallot, finely chopped
4 cloves of garlic, crushed
sprig of fresh thyme, finely chopped
½ lb crumbled goat's cheese
salt and pepper to taste

1. In medium sized sauté pan, melt butter. Add shallots, chili, garlic, thyme and mushrooms. Sauté on high heat until mushrooms and shallots are soft.
2. Place heart toasts on baking sheet and top with mushroom mixture. Sprinkle with goat's cheese.
3. Broil for 2-3 minutes or until Parmesan cheese has completely melted and just started to brown. Cool for 3-5 minutes and serve warm.

Makes approximately 40 Mushroom and Goats Cheese Toasts.

Marry when the year is new.
Always loving, kind and true.
When February birds do mate
You may wed, nor dread your fate.
If you wed when March winds blow,
Joy and sorrow both you'll know.
Marry in April when you can,
Joy for maiden and for man.
Marry in the month of May
You will surely rue the day.
Marry when June roses blow,
Over land and sea you'll go.
Those who in July do wed
Labor always for their bread.
Whoever wed in August be
Many a change is sure to see.
Marry in September's shrine
Your living will be rich and fine.
If in October you do marry,
Love will come but riches tarry.
If you wed in bleak November
Only joy will come, remember.
When December's snows fall fast,
Marry and true love will last.

GROOM'S GIFT: THE BOOK OF US

12–24 sheets of 8 ½" x 11" lightweight card stock, 2 sheets of 9" x 11 ½" heavy-weight card stock, two pieces of 9 ½" x 11 ½" decorative fabric or leather, hole punch, scissors, craft glue, 1–2 yards of ribbon or leather cord, various colored or handmade papers, vellum or cellophane, self-adhesive photo corners

YOUR FIRST TOOTH, his first step, your bad teenage hair days, his class picture, your first date together, his first bouquet of flowers to you, your first love letter to him. You can display your early years apart and relive the romantic memories of how your lives came together in a special scrapbook that preserves the keepsakes of your past and your present, while allowing adequate space for your future. Surprise your fiancé by having it delivered to him on the morning of your wedding.

- Buy an album-style blank book from your local stationer or follow these simple instructions to make your own:

- Cut a dozen or so pages of lightweight card stock paper to the desired length and width of your scrapbook. Use a hole punch to create two or three holes along the short side of the pages.

- To make the front and back cover for your scrapbook, cut two pages of heavyweight card stock about a 1/4 inch wider and longer than your inside pages. Then cut two rectangles of fabric or leather about 1/2 inch wider than your cover pieces. Brush craft glue on one side of each piece and cover with fabric. Fold the edges of the fabric on the other side and glue in place. After the glue has dried, punch holes in the front and back covers to line up with the inside pages.
- To bind the book, string lengths of ribbon, cord, or leather through the holes and tie a knot and bow.
- Conspire with your fiancé's family to get photographs of his cutest (and most embarrassing!) moments *pre-you,* and dig through your family archives to find photographic evidence of your own similar moments.
- Gather together movie stubs, tickets and programs from sports and entertainment events, menus from favorite restaurants, labels from special bottles of wine, romantic notes, letters and postcards, pressed flowers, ribbons, a selection of photographs, and other mementos from your dating days.
- Arrange your graphic timelines side by side chronologically in the order you want to display them in your scrapbook.

- Using craft glue and old-fashioned photo corners, affix your momentos to the pages of your scrapbook. Add hand-written captions including dates and descriptions.

- To make pockets in your scrapbook for your courtship memories, cut various-sized squares of card stock. Create an aesthetic look with opaque or colored paper, handmade paper, or paper made with flower petals. Glue or sew paper squares in place along the bottom and side edges. For see-through pockets, try using vellum or heavyweight cellophane. Affix small envelopes with glue in your scrapbook to store love letters or poems. Begin the scrapbook with a private letter to your fiancé, to be read the morning of your wedding.

- If you wish to add to your scrapbook once you are married, just add pages and replace ribbons with longer pieces, if necessary.

To keep your marriage brimming,
With love in the loving cup,
Whenever you're wrong, admit it;
Whenever you're right, shut up.

Ogden Nash

Thanks to a love-struck Dutch maiden, modern brides are showered with gifts and surprises before they are wed. According to folklore, the custom began some three hundred years ago when the daughter of a well-to-do Dutchman fell in love with a miller. He was a good man, but her father disapproved, for the miller was poor from giving flour away to the less fortunate. When the bride's father refused to give his daughter a dowry, her friends and neighbors showered her with enough gifts and blessings so that she could marry her true love after all.

Showering the bride

Ever since, friends of brides-to-be regularly descend upon the bride and load her with advice, good luck, and presents that will start her off in her new home and new life. In the 1890s, it became fashionable to place gifts for the new bride into a Japanese parasol. Later the bride was "showered" with presents as the parasol was opened over her head. Another popular Victorian container for shower gifts was a crepe-paper wishing well.

THROUGHOUT EUROPE AND AFRICA, brides have commonly packed a trousseau, or "bottom drawer," filled with linens, clothing, and jewels. Neighbors in colonial America frequently gathered for a quilting bee, an all-day event during which they'd sew a quilt with a double wedding ring or other nuptial pattern. In Lithuania, the night before the wedding, the bride's closest friends bestow her with handwoven articles and spend the night helping her pack her hope chest. Many elder African village women will "load the bride" with words of wisdom and household goods.

SHOWERS OFTEN COME AS A SURPRISE to the bride, who can expect to be subjected to a fair amount of good-natured fun and games. Gift givers who know that each broken ribbon foretells a baby might go out of their way to wrap presents with extra ties and tape to make sure the bride will have to cut or rip them. In times past, a bridesmaid might have gathered all the ribbons into a pillow to keep in the newlyweds' home for continual good luck. Now a bridesmaid often ties all the ribbons together into a mock bouquet to use during the wedding rehearsal.

A Hurry of Showers

Green Thumb: An informal picnic luncheon where guests shower the bride with garden tools, seeds, bulbs, plants, and garden ornaments. Guests may also plant a bridal wreath for the lucky couple.

Nest Builder: Fill the bride's linen closets with tablecloths, lace napkins, napkin holders, towels, place mats, bed sheets, duvet covers, pillows, and pillowcases.

Around the world: Each guest is assigned a country and then brings a gift reflecting that culture. For example, Italy might buy a pasta maker or pizza stone; Japan, a wok or cookbook; and England, a set of teacups and fine teas.

'Round the Clock: Assign each guest a time of day on the invitation and inform them that the gift they choose should correspond to that time—7 A.M. could be an alarm clock or bathroom accessories; 10 A.M. might be a coffeemaker or coffee mugs; lunchtime, cooking utensils or a salad bowl; bedtime, lingerie or linens, etc.

Evening of Beauty & Bliss: Guests bring candles, beauty products, spa certificates, and even classic movies for an evening of soothing music, soft aromatic candlelight, and spa fare—designed to help the bride feel relaxed, pampered, and beautiful.

Recipe Round-up: A potluck lunch or dinner where each guest brings a special dish, its recipe, and a gift to help stock the bride's kitchen. Include a blank recipe card with the invitation then collect the filled-in cards into a recipe box at the shower.

GRANDMOTHER'S QUILT

RETOLD FROM A STORY BY ANNIE F. S. BEARD

As a young girl growing up in Cleveland, Ohio, I was especially enchanted by Grandmother Barkin's most cherished possession, a quilt she had made with swatches from the wedding gowns of generations of brides in our family.

When company would come for tea, Grandmother would spread out the quilt, enthralling her guests and especially me with her tales of each delicate piece and the bride who wore it. The well-to-do brides in our family left behind swatches of silk, satin, brocade, and velvet, while the pioneer brides of lesser means contributed their soft muslin and calico. A piece from Grandmother's own wedding gown was proudly displayed in the center of the quilt, where she had embroidered "Love One Another" atop the fading blue satin.

To my delight, Grandmother would often smile sweetly and say, "This wedding quilt will be yours one day, dear Mary." Since Grandmother had only sons and no daughter and I was the eldest granddaughter, the quilt would be passed down to me if I married first.

Although I was approaching twenty-five, I was more concerned with the kind of man I wanted to marry than getting married just for the sake of getting married. I sincerely doubted I would ever own the quilt until my childhood friend Leonard Wynn and I began to take the same path to work each day.

As Leonard and I would wind our way through the narrow streets leading to town, he would amuse me with his stories. However, one crisp fall day in 1861 any hope of our romance developing was dashed when he informed me he had enlisted in the Union army. When the day came to see him off at the train station, I felt as though my heart would break.

The enthusiasm and patriotic spirit of the women of Cleveland reached a zenith during the Civil War. And Grandmother Barkin and I were no exception. Freely and abundantly Grandmother sent supplies from her stores. But her crowning sacrifice was yet to be made.

Early one bright winter morning a carriage rolled up to Grandmother's door, and out of it stepped two eager young ladies who took Grandmother aside and said in whispered tones, "So you see, Mrs. Barkin, we are desperate for quilts for our soldiers." Slowly rising from her chair, the elderly lady stood and then proceeded to her wardrobe. Out came her treasured quilt, wrapped in white and fragrant with lavender. Calling to me, she said, "Mary, they need quilts at the hospital. I have no other ready-made ones. Are you willing to give this one up?"

I hesitated for only a moment, realizing that every gift added one more chance of comfort for my Leonard.

So Grandmother's quilt adorned one of the cots in the hospital and gave warmth and pleasure to many a poor sufferer, serving a purpose far greater than its maker had intended.

Grandmother and I joined the tireless group at the Cleveland hospital. One Christmas as I was passing from cot to cot distributing grapes and oranges, I watched the eager looks of the poor fellows. Having emptied my basket, I went to assist in feeding those who were unable to help themselves.

Taking a plate of jelly in my hand, I stepped to the side of one of the cots, noticing as I did that Grandmother's quilt lay upon the bed! The sight of it brought a rush of tender memories, filling my eyes with tears so that for a moment I didn't see the face upon the pillow.

Then, with a start, I saw Leonard Wynn. As I dried my eyes, I got a closer look at the white face with sunken eyes revealing the depth of his pain. "No, it can't be," I assured myself.

But the familiar voice erased all doubt. "Ah, Mary, I've been watching and waiting for you!"

Overjoyed I asked, "Why didn't you send for me?"

"I knew you would come sometime. The sight of this," he said, touching the quilt, "made me sure of it."

During the next few weeks, we rediscovered the joys of our companionship. That happiness was quickly extinguished, however, when I arrived at the hospital early one morning to find Leonard's bed occupied by another wounded soldier. A nurse informed me that Leonard had returned to his regiment. Along with Leonard, Grandmother's quilt had also vanished. And so, the Christmas of 1862 came and went, bringing with it joyous surprise only to snatch it and Grandmother's quilt away.

Another long year passed. I was as busy as ever, assisting the cause by trying to impart the Christmas spirit to the soldiers in the hospital. One evening at the close of the day's proceedings, I wearily laid my head down on a table. It was quickly growing dark, and I closed my eyes to snatch, if possible, a brief interval of much needed rest.

Suddenly I was startled. How long had I been asleep, and what was this lying under my head? One glance revealed Grandmother's quilt. How did it get there? I squealed with delight as I heard a familiar voice—Leonard's. "I've come for my Christmas gift, sweet Mary," he said as he drew the quilt to his chest and pointed to the inscription, "Love one another." "I wanted to ask you a year ago but decided that I would not ask you to take a maimed, sick soldier. I kept the quilt in memory of you. See, I fixed it so it would come back to you if anything happened to me." He showed me the label fastened securely to the quilt: "To be sent to Miss Mary Barkin, Cleveland, Ohio."

Then he told me how on one cold winter's day the quilt had saved his life. While sitting close to the fire to warm himself and to cook some potatoes, a stray ball from the enemy's batteries came whistling through the air, taking a straight course toward him. Luckily he was wrapped in the quilt. The ball struck him but, because of the thickness of the quilt, got no further than his coat.

That night Grandmother's quilt went back to its original owner, and my right to it as a wedding gift was firmly established by Leonard's proposal.

From head to toe, virtually every accessory the bride wears on her wedding day is rife with superstition. Here are some age-old ways women have secured their good luck on the way to the altar:

Something old, something new, something borrowed,

WHEN A BRIDE wears something old, such as an heirloom, it's a link to her family roots. Something new is a show of optimism about what is to come. The good fortune of a happily married woman is sure to rub off on a new bride when she wears borrowed jewels or accessories.

THE COLOR BLUE is a symbol of purity and fidelity according to the Old Testament. Ancient Israelites were among the first to wear blue on wedding days.

TO WEAR A VEIL is certain to shield the bride from the Evil Eye. Many African brides have their hair braided to be worn as a veil.

GREEK BRIDES tuck a sugar cube inside a glove to ensure sweetness throughout marriage.

Colonial brides carried a small pouch with a coin, a breadcrumb, wood, and cloth to be sure they'd always have money, food, shelter, and clothing.

Swedish brides leave their shoes unfastened during their wedding ceremonies in the hopes that childbirth will come easily.

something blue and a silver sixpence in your shoe

To make sure they'll never be without happiness or wealth, brides throughout Europe and America slip a coin in their shoes.

A lucky horseshoe strewn with ribbons is a favored totem of Irish brides.

The best and most beautiful things in the world cannot be seen or even touched. They must be felt with the heart.

HELEN KELLER

A ROOM WITH A VIEW

E. M. FORSTER

"YOU MUST MARRY, or your life will be wasted. You have gone too far to retreat. I have no time for the tenderness, and the comradeship, and the poetry, and the things that really matter, and *for which* you marry. I know that, with George, you will find them and that you love him. Then be his wife. He is already part of you. Though you fly to Greece, and never see him again, or forget his very name, George will work in your thoughts till you die. It isn't possible to love and to part. You will wish that it was. You can transmute love, ignore it, muddle it, but you can never pull it out of you...love is eternal....

"I only wish poets would say this, too: love is of the body; not the body but of the body. Ah! the misery that would be saved if we confessed that!...When I think what life is, and how seldom love is answered by love— Marry him; it is one of the moments for which the world was made...."

On your wedding day, beauty and flowers will surround you. Your dearest friends and relatives, your personal "ladies in waiting," will lavish their attention upon you alone. If you're having a traditional wedding, you'll probably deck your bridesmaids out in matching gowns that complement the style and décor of the big event. But just how did this custom of look-alike bridesmaids originate?

Always a bridesmaid, never a bride

IN THE WESTERN TRADITION, the practice of surrounding the bride with similarly dressed young women started as a defense against the bride-stealing Anglo-Saxon and Germanic marauders. The earliest bridesmaids often dressed identically to the bride, in the same color gowns—including veils—to act as decoys and confuse potential kidnappers.

What of the groom's best man? In days of yore, he was generally the right-hand man of the thieving tribesman, ready to assist in snatching the unsuspecting "bride elect." Additional comrades ensured a successful raid for the groom and, if they were lucky, might steal a bride of their own.

It was also once believed that surrounding the bride with a flock of bridesmaids would ward off harmful spirits who might place a curse on the bride and groom's happiness. Early Greek maidens often wed at age fifteen, and tradition called for these young brides to be escorted by a train of happily married, fertile women who served the dual purpose of protecting the bride from evil and allowing their own good fortune to rub off on her.

In some cases, bridal parties took extreme measures, dressing like men to protect themselves against misfortune. In Denmark, the bride and groom changed sex roles to ensure a successful wedding. One ancient Jewish tradition called for the bride to be clad in full armor, complete with helmet and weaponry.

ATTENDANT GIFTS

THEY'LL STAND BY YOUR SIDE through tears and laughter and make certain you look radiant on your wedding day. It's only natural for you to do something special for your attendants to thank them for all their support and comfort during your engagement and wedding. The custom of the bride bestowing gifts on her bridesmaids is centuries old. Traditionally, the bride paid for the gloves her attendants wore during the ceremony. Nowadays, the bride might give her bridesmaids jewelry or hair accessories that they can wear on the wedding day. Whether you choose classic or modern gifts will depend on what you think your attendants will appreciate most.

For a personal touch, consider giving your bridesmaids a handmade gift they can use for your wedding and many occasions to come. Handkerchief purses are easy to sew and an elegant way to say thank you. Begin by looking for antique handkerchiefs or linen napkins with embroidered borders or lace trim. Choose complementary decorative ribbons to use as handles.

HANDMADE HANDKERCHIEF PURSE

Antique handkerchief or linen napkin, thread, pins, 18-inch length of satin ribbon

1. Starch and press handkerchief.

2. Lay handkerchief wrong side down and fold the bottom half up to meet the top edge. Pin the sides together.

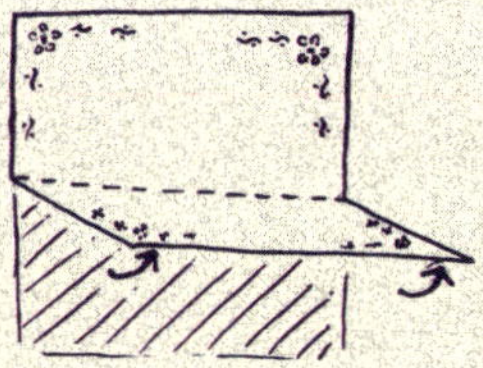

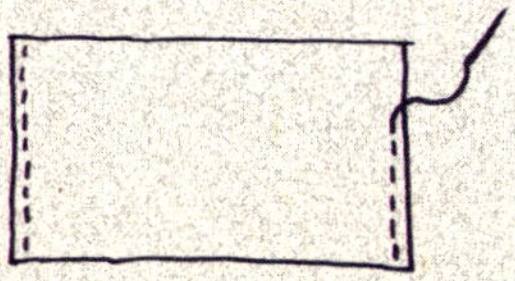

3. Sew the sides by machine or by hand with a backstitch.

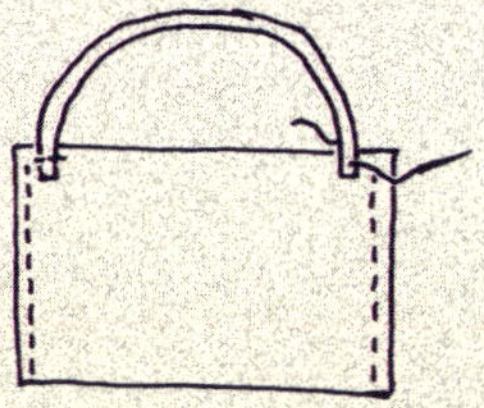

4. Pin ribbon ends to the inside seams and sew in place.

5. Turn the bag inside out and press.

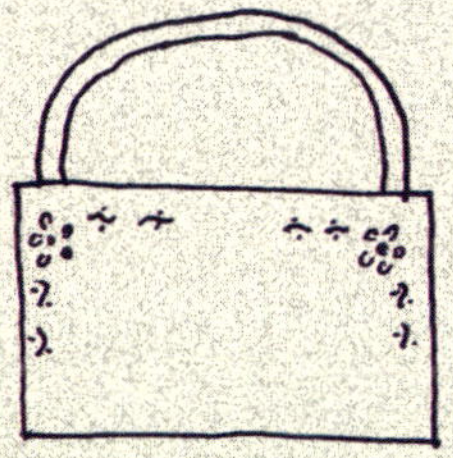

If time is running out or you're just not the crafty type, here are some attendant gift suggestions that are both personal and readily available at most department and specialty stores:

ENGRAVED SILVER MIRRORS, COMPACTS, OR PICTURE FRAMES ❦ EARRINGS TO WEAR AT THE WEDDING ❦ SPA GIFT CERTIFICATES ❦ CRYSTAL BUD VASES ❦ LEATHER JOURNALS OR PHOTO ALBUMS ❦ SILK SCARVES ❦ PERFUME ATOMIZERS ❦ LINGERIE ❦ FOUNTAIN PENS ❦ TICKETS TO THE THEATER, A CONCERT, OR A SPORTING EVENT

BRIDAL TEA PARTY

In the busy days before your wedding, hosting a "girls only" bridesmaids' luncheon can be a welcome break for you and your attendants. Such occasions are ideal opportunities to thank your bridesmaids with individual gifts and an appetizing array of food. The menu for a bridal tea includes finger sandwiches and salads, most of which can be prepared a day ahead. In addition to an assortment of teas, you may want to offer sherry or champagne cocktails.

A mismatched tea set is a charming option for an informal luncheon, and if you plan to serve several different kinds of tea, you'll be using different pots anyway! Rifle through antique shops, flea markets, thrift stores, and sales at home and department stores for a variety of pretty, quality teapots, teacups, and saucers with no cracks. After lunch, wash and pack all the cups and saucers (don't forget to have some newspaper or tissue paper handy) and present each bridesmaid with one as a souvenir.

MENU SUGGESTIONS

TEA SERVICE

assorted loose black and herbal teas
cinnamon sticks
lemon and orange slices
honey
sugar cubes
cream and milk

To make the perfect pot of tea, start with cold, freshly drawn water. Bring water to a rolling boil and immediately pour a small amount in the teapot. Swirl the hot water around to warm the teapot, then discard. Place one teaspoon of tea leaves per cup of water into the teapot, then pour the water over the leaves. Steep for 3 to 5 minutes. Pour tea through a small strainer to serve.

FINGER SANDWICHES

cucumber & cream cheese
tomato & herbed butter
salmon, cream cheese, & dill
watercress & cream cheese
thinly sliced turkey & Dijon mustard-cranberry sauce spread
prosciutto & melon slices
aged cheddar & tomato

Remove the crusts from an assortment of light and dark slices of bread. Spread with herbed butter or cream cheese and various toppings. Then halve or quarter the slices to make bite-size tea sandwiches.

SWEET TREATS

fresh fruit salad
shortbread
currant scones
lemon poundcake
petit fours

A proper high tea always includes something sweet to balance the savory. If you include breakfast breads, be sure to offer butter and strawberry jam.

CHARM CAKE

Treat your attendants to a sweet slice of fortune with their tea and bake a Victorian-style bridesmaids' cake embedded with silver charms attached to long ribbons. According to lore, the bride should sift the flour with her own hands to infuse the cake with her good luck. Before the cake is cut, each bridesmaid pulls a ribbon to discover what future her charm predicts. Shop local yard sales and jewelry stores for inexpensive silver charms.

Typical Charms and Their Meanings:

airplane = travel
anchor = life of stability
baby buggy = children
clover = good luck
flowers = blossoming love
heart = true love will find you
key = happy home
knot = steadfast love
money tree = life of riches
ring = next engaged
rocking chair = long life
telephone = good news
wishing well = granted wish
wreath = contented life

FOR CAKE:

1 stick (1/2 cup) butter
1 1/4 cups sugar
1 cup milk
1 tablespoon vanilla
2 1/4 cups pastry flour
2 1/2 teaspoons baking powder
1/4 teaspoon salt
4 egg whites

1. Preheat oven to 375° F.
2. In large bowl, cream butter and sugar until light and fluffy. Add milk and vanilla and mixed until blended.
3. In separate bowl, sift flour, baking powder, and salt. Add to wet mixture in thirds. After each addition, stir the batter until smooth.
4. Whip egg whites until stiff. Fold into batter.
5. Pour batter evenly into two greased 9-inch round cake pans. Bake for about 25 minutes or until tester comes out clean. Allow to cool completely on racks before frosting.

FOR ICING:

1 stick (1/2 cup) unsalted butter
3 1/2 cups confectioner's sugar
3 tablespoons whipping cream
1 lemon rind, grated
1/2 teaspoon orange extract

1. In medium bowl, cream butter and sugar together until smooth.
2. Beat in whipping cream.
3. Add lemon rind and orange extract and mix until blended.
4. With a spatula, spread icing on top of first layer of cake. Stack second layer on top and spread remaining icing over sides of cake.
5. Arrange charms evenly around the top layer of cake. Gently press charms into the cake with your fingertip. Then carefully ice the top of the cake, leaving ribbons exposed.

Tip: To prevent ribbons from getting iced while you work, wrap them in plastic wrap or aluminum foil. Remove the wrap prior to serving.

Go seek her out all courteously,
And say I come,
Wind of spices whose song is ever
Epithalamium.
O hurry over the dark lands
And run upon the sea
For seas and land shall not divide us
My love and me.

Now, wind, of your good courtesy
I pray you go,
And come into her little garden
And sing at her window;
Singing: The bridal wind is blowing
For Love is at his noon;
And soon will your true love be with you,
Soon, O soon.

POEM XIII FROM *CHAMBER MUSIC*
James Joyce

On her wedding day, the bride leaves behind her old life, ready to embark upon her new status as a married woman. To bridge that transition, cultures throughout the world partake in cleansing and beautifying rituals that start the bride off on the right foot. Many such customs are performed with the aid of married women, with the belief that their good fortune will rub off on the new bride.

Preparing the bride for her walk down the aisle

BODY ART

As part of several days of premarital preparation, Moroccan and Egyptian women immerse themselves in specially prepared milk baths and have body hair removed with a homemade lemon-sugar depilatory recipe. They, as well as Muslim women in India, Nigeria, and Ethiopia, are treated to full-body massages with coconut or olive oil. Finally, professional henna artists paint their hands and feet with elaborate designs. The artwork lasts for several days and is believed to keep malevolent spirits at bay.

In other parts of the world, brides have their faces adorned to greet their new husbands. Korean women have red dots painted on their cheeks and foreheads. Masai women decorate their faces and hair with red ocher dye. And in Indonesia, brides are beautified with patterns of white dots on their cheeks, noses, and foreheads.

RITUAL BATH

In China, the day before her wedding, a bride takes a purifying herbal bath prepared with bamboo, pine, and the pungent herb artemisia, so that her married life may be long, prosperous, and strong. Young Jewish women partake in a special bath called a mikvah, in which the elder women of the community participate. The bride to be is immersed several times in a special pool or natural body of water and recites a blessing for spiritual purification. She emerges from the water "born anew" to cross the sacred threshold into marriage. Navaho women also come together to prepare the bride with a ritual bath and help her dress for her nuptials. A Hopi mother will wash her daughter's hair with yucca root to purify her on her wedding day.

FOOD OF LOVE

While American brides typically lose weight in preparation for their wedding day, some brides in Nigeria, Togo, and Tanzania spend weeks eating specially made foods to fatten up so they may be voluptuous, fertile, and beautiful for their new husbands.

Marry when the sun doth shine

Once you spread the news that you're getting married, most everyone will have a bit of advice about what ensures good luck on the Big Day. If you find a spider on your wedding gown, you'll come into money. If you marry on the incoming tide, you'll have prosperity. If you see a flock of birds, your marriage will be blessed with fertility. If it snows, you'll be wealthy. If the sun is out, you'll be a happy bride. These tried-and-true Old Wives' tales may help you garner all the luck possible on your wedding day.

DO

- Marry under a waxing moon so happiness will grow.
- Marry as the hands of the clock move up (after the half hour) for good fortune.
- Throw away all the pins from your bridal wear after the wedding for a long marriage.

and you'll be a happy bride

DON'T

- Wear the complete wedding attire before the wedding day.
- Look in the mirror before walking down the aisle, lest you leave any part of yourself behind.
- Allow the groom to see you in your dress before the wedding. It's bad luck to see the future before it happens.
- Drop the ring during the ceremony, or else it's best to start over.
- Wear the wedding ring before the wedding day.
- Shed tears before the kiss. To cry on your wedding day prevents tears during the marriage.
- Invite an even number of guests to attend the ceremony.
- Feed a cat out of your wedding shoe for good luck.
- Kiss a chimney sweep if you see one on your wedding day. You'll have good luck throughout your marriage.
- Sew a penny into the seam of your wedding dress for luck on your wedding day and prosperity in your wedded life.

THE PAMPERED BRIDE

ON HER WEDDING DAY, a bride deserves to look and feel like a queen. Treat yourself to an at-home spa in the days leading up to your wedding to bring out your most beautiful self. Try these easy steps to overnight radiance.

- Soak away pre-wedding tension with a bath of Epsom salts and lavender. Add 3 cups of Epsom salts and 1 cup finely ground lavender buds to a bath of warm water. Exfoliate with a body brush and finish off by massaging coconut oil into your skin for ultimate softness.
- Revive fatigued and sensitive skin with rose water. Boil a white rose and gently rub the petals into your face until the moisture vaporizes. Or, treat yourself to a facial by mixing 2 tablespoons rose water, 2 tablespoons yogurt, 1 tablespoon honey, and 2 tablespoons dried rose petals and lavender, crumbled. Dab the mixture onto your face and relax. After 20 minutes, rinse and pat dry.
- Make your lips even more kissable with a soft-bristled toothbrush. Gently brush your lips to rub away dry or dead skin and leave them ever so smooth.

- Soothe your dry eyes with the cooling properties of cucumber. A few hydrating slices on your eyes really do help hide delicate lines. When tears of joy leave your eyes red and puffy, calm them with moistened chamomile tea bags.

- Give yourself shiny, voluminous hair with a protein-packed egg and avocado conditioner. Mix one egg and half of an avocado and massage into hair and scalp. Leave in for at least 20 minutes before rinsing.

- Your overworked hands deserve some special attention for the moment your groom places your wedding band on your finger. Blend 1 tablespoon honey, 1 tablespoon almond oil, and $3/4$ teaspoon lemon juice. Rub the mixture into your skin and rest for

STRESS-FREE EMERGENCY PACK

Avoid last-minute mishaps by preparing a basket in the bridal suite for you and your bridesmaids. Include:

ASPIRIN ❧ BAND-AIDS ❧ CHALK OR WHITE MEDICAL TAPE (FOR HIDING SMUDGES ON WHITE FABRIC) ❧ CLEAR NAIL POLISH (FOR SNAGGED HOSIERY) ❧ COMPACT POWDER ❧ EMERY BOARD ❧ GUM OR MINTS ❧ HAIRBRUSH ❧ HAIR SPRAY ❧ LIPSTICK OR LIP BALM ❧ LOTION ❧ NEEDLE & THREAD ❧ NOTEPAD & PEN ❧ SAFETY PINS ❧ TISSUES

about 10 minutes. Rinse with warm water for soft, sweet-smelling skin.

- You'll be standing on them all day long, so give your feet some extra love before you walk down the aisle. Make a heel-to-toe softening foot scrub by mixing 2 cups sea salt, 2 tablespoons dried, chopped orange peel, 3 drops essential oil of lavender, and 3 drops essential oil of tea tree. Gently massage into your feet during a bath or shower.

Marry in gray,
you will go far away.
Married in black,
you will wish yourself back.
Married in brown,
you will live out of town.
Married in red,
you will wish yourself dead.
Married in pearl,
you will live in a whirl.
Married in green,
ashamed to be seen.
Married in yellow,
ashamed of your fellow.
Married in blue,
he will always be true.
Married in pink,
your spirits will sink.
Married in white
you have chosen alright.

All eyes will be upon you on your wedding day. What you wear will be part of the treasured moments captured in everyone's memories for years to come. But did you know that the flowing white wedding gown is a relatively modern convention from nineteenth-century England?

Married in white

Before Victorian times, women wore their "Sunday best" dresses, which were generally light blue, lilac, rose, or pale yellow. Many brides would simply sew on additional trim or lace to make their dresses more special. Whatever the shade, the superstitious bride adhered to the custom of putting the last stitches in her gown just before walking down the aisle. This ensured that her happiness, like her gown, could not be complete until she married. Brides in other parts of the world still wear color, and lots of it:

Spanish Roman Catholic brides have traditionally worn wedding attire of **BLACK** silk with a matching lace mantilla. The gown is dedicated to an image of the Virgin Mary after the wedding.

GREEN, considered by many brides to be an unlucky color, is a favorite choice for Norwegian brides.

Nepalese and Indian brides wear **GOLD**-threaded saris on their wedding days.

you have chosen all right

The traditional colors woven into the Native American bride's dress indicate the four directions of the Earth—**BLACK** for north, **BLUE** for south, **WHITE** for east, and **YELLOW** for west.

In China and Japan, **RED** has long been a traditional color of good luck, vitality, and life. Chinese brides wear ornate gowns embroidered with golden Phoenixes. Instead of veils, they wear elaborate headdresses made of kingfisher feathers, pearls, and gilded silver. The number of layers in the kimono worn by Japanese brides indicates her class. Royalty wear as many as twelve layers, whereas commoners wear only three. Traditionally, a Japanese bride wears an obi or dagger in her sash. She'll also wear a white headpiece to hide "the horns of jealousy" that all women supposedly possess.

Bulgarian brides still favor the traditional aladza dress, often passed down from generation to generation. The dress is hand woven of wool or silk in a pattern of dark red stripes on a **RED**, **WHITE**, **YELLOW**, or **SKY BLUE** background, depending on the season. Opening like a coat, it is worn over a tunic-shaped smock of handwoven white cotton cloth finished in lace along the hem and sleeves. The bride wears a decorative apron of silk or wool in shades of red and green, with wide lace trim.

BLUE—the ancient color of purity, love, and fidelity—is popular with Irish, Amish, and Jewish brides. For her first wedding, Mary, Queen of Scots, wore a spectacular dark blue velvet gown decorated with jewels and white embroidery.

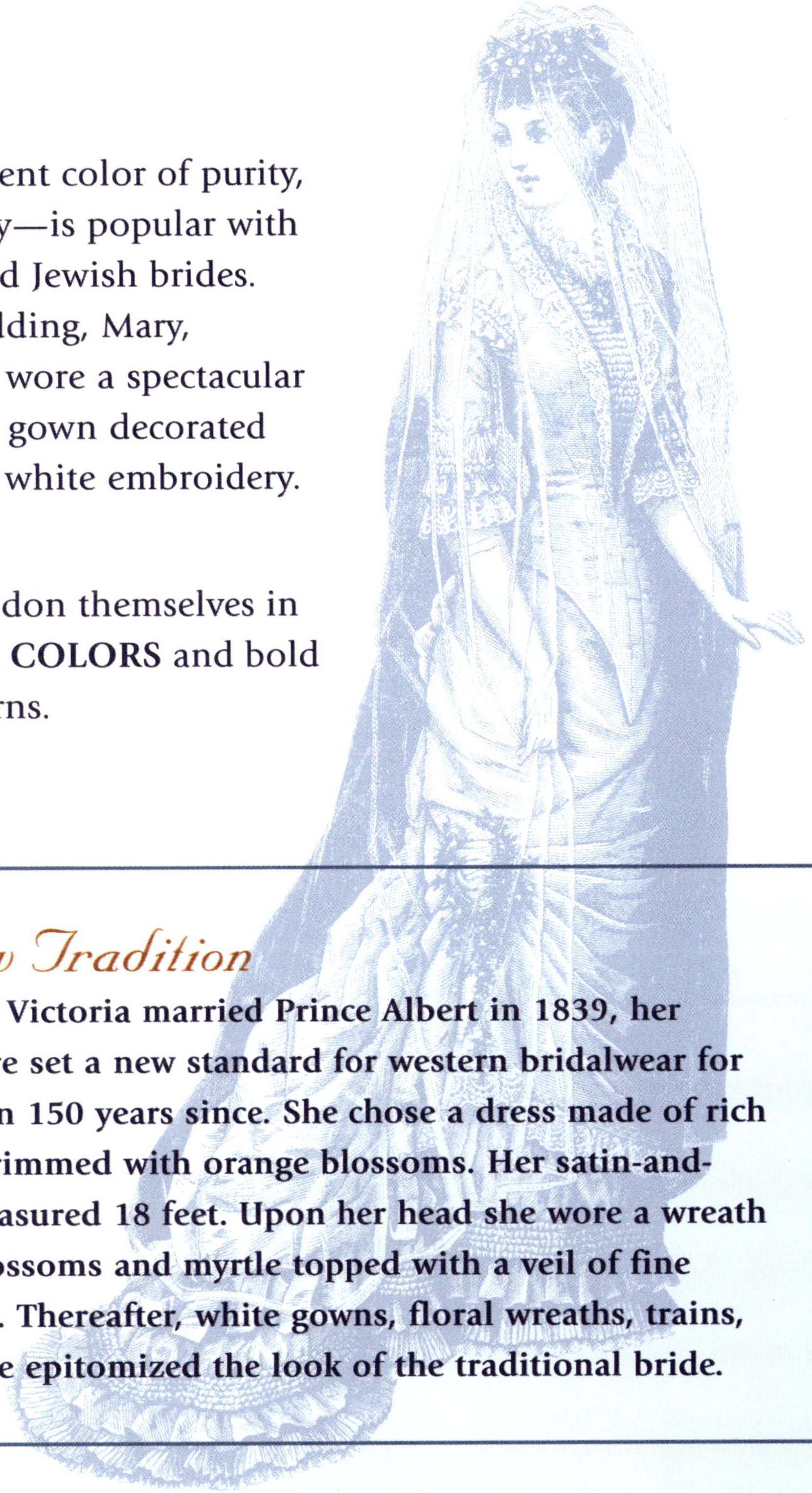

Nigerian brides don themselves in bright, **FESTIVE COLORS** and bold geometric patterns.

The New Tradition

When Queen Victoria married Prince Albert in 1839, her wedding attire set a new standard for western bridalwear for the more than 150 years since. She chose a dress made of rich white satin trimmed with orange blossoms. Her satin-and-lace train measured 18 feet. Upon her head she wore a wreath of orange blossoms and myrtle topped with a veil of fine Honiton lace. Thereafter, white gowns, floral wreaths, trains, and veils have epitomized the look of the traditional bride.

In our life there is a single color, as on an artist's palette, which provides the meaning of life and art. It is the color of love.

MARC CHAGALL

FLORAL ADORNMENTS

A SIMPLE FLOWER can put the perfect finishing touch on any member of your bridal party. In addition to complementing the color scheme of your wedding, flowers add romantic symbolism to the event and elegance to those who wear them. You may decide to adorn junior bridesmaids or flower girls with wreaths of white rosebuds for innocence, or groomsmen with boutonnieres of evergreen berries for longevity.

HEAD WREATH

Measuring tape, florist's wire, florist's tape, wire cutters, flowers and foliage of choice, assorted ribbons

1. Measure the circumference of the wearer's head and cut a piece of florist's wire about two inches longer. Make a wire hoop by overlapping the wire ends by a $1/2$ inch and wrapping them together with florist's tape.

2. Trim the fresh flower and greenery stems, leaving about two inches of stem below each bloom or leaf. Bundle

together 2 or 3 cut stems. Run a 5-inch length of wire along the stems and make a hairpin bend just beneath the buds. Wrap the remaining length of wire around the stems several times, spiraling downward.

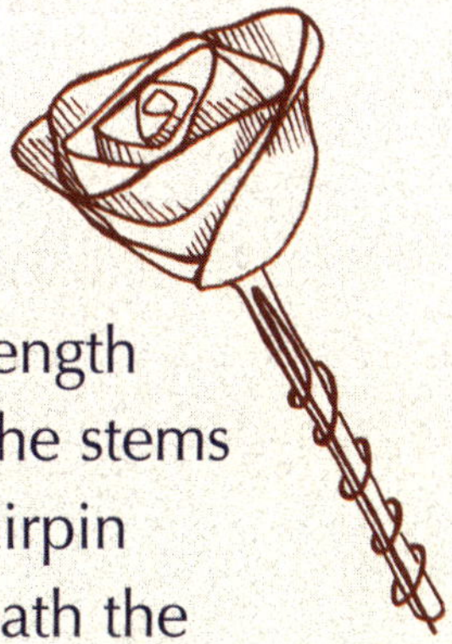

3. Evenly arrange the wired flowers and foliage around the wreath so that they are overlapping a little, and wrap the stem extensions onto the headdress using florist's tape.

4. Decorate with ribbons and bows, if you like.

BOUTONNIERE

Flowers and foliage of choice, florist's wire, florist's tape, measuring tape, wire cutters, satin ribbon, antique straight pin

1. Begin with one or two sprigs of foliage and a single flower.
2. Trim the stems to desired length and wrap with florist's wire as in Step 2 of Head Wreath.
3. Wrap the wired stems in florist's tape.
4. Wrap decorative ribbon around the stems and finish with a simple knot or bow. Attach the boutonniere to a lapel with an antique straight pin.

As symbols of beauty and fertility, bridal bouquets have been a central part of wedding ceremonies for centuries. In early England, the bride was thought to be imbued with the power to transmit good fortune. Hoping for a little luck, spectators tore away bits of her clothing and grabbed for her fortuitous flowers, ribbons, and headdress. In self-defense, the bride often tossed her bouquet!

A bundle of flowers

Perfumed bouquets have warded off sickness as well as provided homage to the sweetness of marriage, while aromatic nosegays of garlic, herbs, and grains were thought to keep evil spirits at bay.

No matter what kind of wedding you have, you can celebrate the floral bouquet tradition and choose from an abundance of meaningful flowers and arrangements:

Arm bouquet: a long, gently curved arrangement of flowers, designed to be cradled in the arm

Cascade: a handheld bouquet that spills down from its base like a waterfall

Nosegay or posie: a circular cluster of upright flowers held by a small handle at its base

Pomander: a ball of densely packed, sweet-smelling herbs and flowers held by a loop of ribbon

Tussie-mussie: a small, spiral posie with fragrant flowers and herbs, usually chosen for their meanings

WHEN YOU SELECT THE FLOWERS FOR YOUR BOUQUETS, you may want to choose varieties for their hidden meanings as well as for their outward beauty. Here's a sampling of the secret language of flowers:

AMARANTH— unfading love

AMARYLLIS— splendid beauty

APPLE BLOSSOM— good fortune

AZALEA— romance

BACHELOR'S BUTTON— hope, love

BLUEBELL— kindness

CLOVER— faithfulness

DAFFODILS AND DAISIES— sunny disposition

EVERGREEN— undying love

FIG— longevity

FORGET-ME-NOT— true love

GARDENIA— joy

HYACINTH— constancy

HYDRANGEA— devotion

IVY— fidelity

JASMINE— sensuality

LILY OF THE VALLEY— purity

MARIGOLDS— sensual passion

MINT— fecundity, virtue

MYRTLE— love, peace, happiness

ORANGE BLOSSOMS— happiness, fertility, everlasting luck

ORCHIDS— beauty, passion

PERIWINKLE— sweet memories

PHLOX— united hearts

PINE— compassion, longevity

POMEGRANATE— fertility

ROSE— love

ROSEMARY— remembrance

SAGE— domestic virtue

THYME— courage

Orange Blossoms

The evergreen orange tree blooms in all seasons, making it a natural choice as a bridal flower. According to Greek myth, Jupiter gave orange blossoms to the goddess Juno on their wedding night, while Gaea, goddess of earth and fertility, presented Hera with a garland of orange blossoms to bless her marriage to Zeus. Legend has it that this first bridal flower made its way to Europe from Saracens by way of the Crusaders. The Spanish have since laid claim to being the first to wear the orange blossom for weddings. Apparently, the daughter of a Spanish king's gardener sold a cutting from an orange tree to a French ambassador in order to earn money for her dowry. The young woman was so grateful to the tree that she wore orange blossoms in her hair on her wedding day as a tribute. The ambassador later presented the cutting to the king of France, who had it planted in his royal garden. The tree that grew is believed to be alive and well at Versailles today.

When Queen Victoria considered what to wear as a crown on her wedding day, she chose a wreath of orange blossoms rather than one of her elaborate jeweled tiaras.

PRESERVING YOUR BOUQUET

PRESERVE YOUR BRIDAL BLOOMS and keep them as a beautiful reminder of your wedding day. Here are some easy ways to make your bouquet last a lifetime.

DRIED BOUQUETS

The simple method for drying flowers is to hang them upside down in a warm, dry room. Keep them out of direct sunlight to minimize fading. They should dry in two to three weeks.

For dried bouquets that will keep their color, place the flowers on a bed of silica gel crystals in an airtight container and carefully arrange the crystals over the flowers until no air gaps are present. Seal container. Remove the crystals as soon as the flowers are dried, in about two days.

PRESSED FLOWERS

Press individual flowers between the pages of a large book and stack several heavy books on top. Allow a few weeks for the flowers to dry. You can display them in an album or frame them along with ribbons from your bouquet.

POTPOURRI

Remove all the petals from your bouquet, spread them out on a flat surface in the sun and leave them to dry for about a week. Transfer petals to a mixing bowl, add a few drops of your favorite scented oil, and toss to evenly distribute. Use your bridal potpourri to make sachets for your fine garment drawers or simply display it in a decorative bowl for all to enjoy.

Choose not alone a proper mate,

Superstitions abound when it comes time for couples to choose the perfect day to wed. Chinese couples know that the first new moon of the year during peach-blossom time is extremely lucky. Others believe that to marry on the full moon is a good omen. Ancient Romans consulted numerology, and in some cases pig's entrails, to determine the best day for a wedding. In England, the groom's birthday is an exceptionally lucky day to marry; the same does not hold true for the bride's. For many, picking the right month is the first step to making sure the marriage starts off on a good note:

The ancient Greeks preferred **JANUARY**, the month dedicated to Hera, wife of Zeus. Fertility rites were common at that time of year, making it a natural time for nuptial celebrations.

FEBRUARY weddings have not always been favored among Catholics. The old English rhyme "Marry in Lent, you'll live to repent" comes from the time the Catholic Church prohibited marriages at that time of year. But according to the Celtic calendar, the first day of spring falls in February, an ideal time for couples to wed.

but a proper time to marry

Couples who marry in **MARCH** may have a belligerent relationship, like the personality of the Roman god Mars, after whom the month is named.

APRIL is ideal for lovers to tie the knot, since that month is hallowed by the Roman goddess of love, Venus.

Queen Victoria prohibited her family members to marry in the unlucky month of **MAY**. That time of year is linked to Lemuria, the Roman Feast of the Dead, during which the ancient Romans were not allowed to bathe or wear festive clothing. Not all shun May, however: It's the time of Beltaine, the Irish festival of life and fertility, when couples dance around the maypole.

The ancient Romans favored **JUNE**, still one of the most popular months to marry. Betrothed couples hoped that Juno, the goddess of women, would bring special blessings to their marriage.

In agrarian communities, people avoided marrying in **JULY** between the time of hay and harvest, to keep needed workers in the fields.

The harvest-reaping month of **AUGUST** kept many from planning wedding days, but in Ireland, it's one of the most popular times to marry. Couples who wed during the early August festival of Lughnassadh are assured of warm companionship throughout the winter months.

Many believe that marrying on the full harvest moon in **SEPTEMBER** will enhance fertility.

The Victorians cautioned, "If in **OCTOBER**, you do marry, love will come, but riches tarry." Depending upon whose advice you seek, some will say that October weddings mean a life full of work, while others insist the harvest month is a harbinger for a fertile marriage.

The ancient Greeks thought luck came to couples who wed during the colder months. An old Irish rhyme celebrates the most abundant time of year for couples to marry: "**NOVEMBER** is said time to wed, the crops is made and no warmth in bed!"

If snow falls on a **DECEMBER** wedding, the couple is sure to have a happy marriage. To marry on the last day of the year is one of the luckiest days of all, for the last memories of the year will be the couple's happiest.

JOURNAL

BY QUEEN VICTORIA

Queen Victoria's journal entries beginning on her wedding day to Albert:

10 February 1840

Got up at ¼ to 9—well, and having slept well; and breakfasted at ½ p. 9. Mamma came before and brought me a Nosegay of orange flowers. My dearest kindest Lehzen gave me a dear little ring...Had my hair dressed and the wreath of orange flowers put on. Saw Albert for the last time alone, as my Bridegroom.

Saw Uncle, and Ernest whom dearest Albert brought up. At ½ p. 12 I set off, dearest Albert having gone before. I wore a white satin gown with a very deep flounce of Honiton lace, Imitation of old. I wore my Turkish diamond necklace and earrings, and Albert's beautiful sapphire brooch....The Ceremony was very imposing, and fine and simple, and I think ought to make an everlasting impression on every one who promises at the Altar to keep what he or she promises. Dearest Albert repeated everything very distinctly. I felt so happy when the ring was put on, and by Albert. As soon as the Service was over, the Procession returned as it came, with the exception that my beloved Albert led me out. The applause was very great, in the Colour Court as we came through; Lord Melbourne, good man, was very much affected during the Ceremony and at the applause...I then returned to Buckingham Palace alone with Albert; they cheered us really most warmly and heartily; the crowd was immense; and the Hall at Buckingham Palace was full of people; they cheered us again and again...I went and sat on the sofa in my dressing-room with

Albert; and we talked together there from 10 m. to 2 till 20 m. p. 2. Then we went downstairs where all the Company was assembled and went into the dining-room—dearest Albert leading me in... Talked to all after the breakfast, and to Lord Melbourne, whose fine coat I praised.

I went upstairs and undressed and put on a white silk gown trimmed with swansdown, and a bonnet with orange flowers. Albert went downstairs and undressed.

As soon as we arrived [at Windsor] we went to our rooms; my large dressing room is our sitting room; the 3 little blue rooms are his... After looking about our rooms for a little while, I went and changed my gown, and then came back to his small sitting room where dearest Albert was sitting and playing; he had put on his windsor coat; he took me on his knee, and kissed me and was so dear and kind. We had our dinner in our sitting room; but I had such a sick headache that I could eat nothing, and was obliged to lie down in the middle blue room for the remainder of the

evening, on the sofa, but, ill or not, I never, never spent such an evening... He called me names of tenderness, I have never yet heard used to me before—was bliss beyond belief! Oh! this was the happiest day of my life!—May God help me to do my duty as I ought and be worthy of such blessings.

11 February 1840

When day dawned (for we did not sleep much) and I beheld that beautiful angelic face by my side, it was more than I can express! He does look so beautiful in his shirt only, with his beautiful throat seen. We got up at ¼ p. 8. When I had laced I went to dearest Albert's room, and we breakfasted together. He had a black velvet jacket on, without any neckcloth on, and looked more beautiful than it is possible for me to say... At 12 I walked out with my precious Angel, all alone—so delightful, on the Terrace and new Walk, arm in arm!... We talked a great deal together. We came home at one, and had luncheon soon after. Poor dear Albert felt sick and uncomfortable, and lay down in my room... He looked so dear, lying there and dozing.

12 February 1840

Already the 2nd day since our marriage; his love and gentleness is beyond everything, and to kiss that dear soft cheek, to press my lips to his, is heavenly bliss. I feel a purer more unearthly feel than I ever did. Oh! was ever woman so blessed as I am.

Had I the heavens' embroidered cloths,
Enwrought with golden and silver light,
The blue and the dim and the dark cloths
Of night and light and the half-light,
I would spread the cloths under your feet:
But I, being poor, have only my dreams;
I have spread my dreams under your feet;
Tread softly because you tread on my dreams.

HE WISHES FOR THE CLOTHS OF HEAVEN
William Butler Yeats

Marriage ceremonies are often abundant with scenic details such as candles, ribbons, unity symbols, and flowers. Virtually every bit of wedding décor is rich with imagery that dates back to antiquity.

Setting the scene for romance

TO SCATTER ROSE PETALS and sweet-smelling herbs on the bridal path is to wish for a future of sweetness and fertility. In days of old, wedding guests would throw grains and wheat along the path to bless the couple with a fruitful and bountiful marriage.

WHEN QUEEN VICTORIA wore a wreath of myrtle and orange blossoms, she was honoring the mythical gods of the Greeks and Romans. Aphrodite, the goddess of love, emerged from the ocean accompanied by nymphs wearing wreaths of myrtle.

Flowers bundled with ribbons and knots harken back to times when lovers literally tied the knot to wed.

Garlands of ivy represent faithfulness and strength, for these hearty vines are difficult to disturb once they've rooted.

The flame from a candle is a reminder of spiritual light, earthly fire, and good wishes for hearth and home. Ancient Romans illuminated their weddings with torches. Young Greek brides are escorted to the altar by candlelight.

Color has always played an important role in weddings: blue for purity, red for vitality, white for innocence, green for fertility and luck.

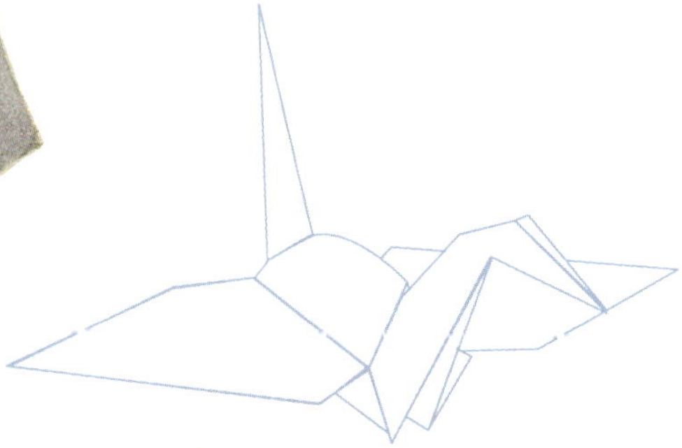

Japanese brides traditionally fold 1001 origami cranes to decorate the wedding hall. Since cranes mate for life, the display of these good-luck birds symbolizes a thousand-fold wish for marital happiness. In Korea, butterfly motifs decorate fans, screens, clothing, and furnishings as symbols of everlasting love and beauty.

GUEST BOOK MEMORIES

Once the official record of all the witnesses at a wedding, the guest book now makes a wonderful keepsake that the bride and groom can revisit over the years to be reminded of the heartfelt wishes from friends and relatives. Instead of having your guests sign their names in a typical journal-style book, invite them to contribute wishes or personal stories that will add to a richer treasury of your wedding day. Consider these ideas:

BOWL OF WISHES

Display a large vase or glass bowl on a prominent table at your reception. Provide small note cards with envelopes and pens that encourage guests to write wishful quips or to wax poetic about you and the groom. Later you can glue the envelopes onto the pages of an empty scrapbook album where you can reopen them to read the cards inside.

PICTORIAL GUEST BOOK

This inventive guest book includes candid photos of all your guests taken at your wedding with a Polaroid camera. Prepare an empty old-fashioned photo album by affixing photo corners throughout to fit the dimensions of the Polaroid stills. Place the album alongside the camera with a small sign instructing each guest to take a picture of themselves, add it to the guest book using the pre-adhered photo corners, and write their wishes and congratulations for the bride and groom below their candid.

MEMORY CARDS

Provide cards in your wedding invitations and ask guests to describe how they met you and/or your groom. When your invitation responses come in the mail, collect all the cards, mount them in a decorative album, and display the book at your reception for others to browse through. It's sure to inspire happy memories.

Nothing is worth more than this day.

GOETHE

Which Finger?

To know if a woman is married, simply look for a ring at the third finger on her left hand, right? Ancient Egyptians did so, but that was not necessarily the norm for everyone. In Ancient Rome, women commonly wore rings on their thumbs. Medieval Gauls and Britons wore rings on their little fingers. And in sixteenth-century England, women wore rings on their right hands. Some Jewish wedding rings are so ornate they're too bulky to wear at all. These rings symbolize the holy temple and serve as ceremonial pieces only, such as a holder for the bride's bouquet.

Perhaps one reason why the third finger of the left hand remains the finger of choice has to do with an old but mistaken belief about anatomy. According to lore, a vein from that finger, aptly named vena amoris, leads directly to the heart. Putting a ring on that finger would keep love from escaping the body.

There's also the medieval Trinitarian formula: During Christian wedding ceremonies, the ring would be placed on the thumb, "in the name of the Father;" on the index finger, "in the name of the Son;" on the middle finger, "in the name of the Holy Spirit;" and, last, on the third finger, "Amen."

On a more practical note, a ring worn on the third finger of the left hand is less likely to get damaged—if you're right-handed.

THE WINGS OF THE DOVE

By Henry James

Set in England in the early 20th century, The Wings of the Dove *is the tragic tale of a love triangle caused by the division of the classes. When Kate falls in love with a poor journalist named Merton, she must choose between her heart and her inheritance. In this scene, she secretly promises herself to Merton.*

AT THIS POINT Kate ceased to attend. He saw after a little that she had been following some thought of her own, and he had been feeling the growth of something determinant even through the extravagance of much of the pleasantry, the warm transparent irony, into which their livelier intimacy kept plunging like a confident swimmer. Suddenly she said to him with extraordinary beauty: "I engage myself to you for ever."

The beauty was in everything, and he could have separated nothing—couldn't have thought of her face as distinct from the whole joy. Yet her face had a new light. "And I pledge you—I call God to witness!—every spark of my faith; I give you every drop of my life." That was all, for the moment, but it was enough, and it was almost as quiet as if it were nothing. They were in the open air, in an alley of the Gardens; the great space, which seemed to arch just then higher and spread wider for them, threw them back into deep concentration. They moved by a common instinct to a spot, within sight, that struck them as fairly sequestered, and there, before their time together was spent, they had extorted from concentration every advance it could make them. They had exchanged vows and tokens, sealed their rich compact, solemnized, so far as breathed words and murmured sounds and lighted eyes and clasped hands could do it, their agreement to belong only, and to belong tremendously, to each other.

I honor your gods

I drink at your well

I bring an undefended heart to our meeting place

I have no cherished outcome

I will not negotiate by withholding

I am not subject to disappointment

CELTIC VOW

To have and to hold,

It's the time everyone is waiting for: the ceremony that will unite the bride and groom as wife and husband. Traditions that have grown out of both common law and religious practices will usually include a processional, a blessing, vows, a unifying ritual such as an exchange of rings, and the nuptial kiss. How this happens is what makes each wedding unique.**

In Jewish weddings, couples come together under the *chuppah*, a canopy that symbolizes the sanctuary of a new home and the spiritual haven the bride and groom will share together. Male members of the congregation hold up each corner of the chuppah during the ceremony. In days of old, traveling bridal parties protected the bride under a canopy en route to meet the groom. Anglo-Saxons held a veil or canopy

from this day forward

called a "care-cloth" over the heads of both the bride and groom while the couple exchanged vows. In China, an elder woman holds an umbrella over the bride's head during the ceremony.

Polynesian bridal couples marry under a bark cloth called a *kapa*. Today, many couples choose to exchange vows under an arbor of flowers in the hope that their marriage will continue to grow and flourish.

Russian Orthodox brides and grooms are crowned king and queen for a day. Witnesses hold silver and gold crowns above the marrying couple's heads during the course of the ceremony. Greek Orthodox couples are crowned with leaves and flowers. The priest leads the couple three times around the altar, after which the bride and groom drink from the same cup of wine to seal their commitment.

Hindu couples take the ceremonial Seven Steps, or *Saptha Padhi*, around a flame together. Each time they pass the flame they make specific promises to each other to enter into a nourishing household blessed with health, wealth, harmony, happiness, children, longevity, and life-long companionship.

Many marrying couples exchange food or drink instead of vows. In Japan and Korea, Shinto ceremonies unite the bride and groom with sake, "the drink of the gods." In a celebration of an old formal bond between two people, the bride and groom take turns drinking three sips from three different sake cups. The order and number of sips vary from village to village. Often the couple's families are invited to drink afterward. In China, couples participate in a tea ceremony. The sweet drink is often specially made with ingredients that connote double meanings, such as dried lily bulbs, or *bok hop*, which also sounds like the phrase that means "a hundred years together." In Nigeria, Yoruban bridal couples share a "tasting of the elements." Both bride and groom take a taste of lemon, vinegar, cayenne pepper, and honey to experience the sour, bitter, hot, and sweet aspects of marriage. In Burma, Buddhist couples place their hands in a bowl of water during the ceremony to symbolize the creation of a union as "indivisible as water."

Not all couples seal their marriage with a kiss. In Hawaii, the bride and groom exchange leis and rub their noses together to celebrate their nuptial bond. Most wedding ceremonies conclude with much cheering and delight. The tradition of church bells, cars honking, or horns or drums playing lives on from the days of old, when people made noise to scare away jealous spirits.

When is a kiss more than a kiss? In ancient Rome, the kiss was legally binding; the public gesture between two betrothed people meant as much as an exchange of rings.

WEDDING KEEPSAKE

THE EXCHANGE OF RINGS is one of the most sacred moments during the wedding ceremony. Make it more meaningful by having the ring bearer deliver your wedding bands on a pillow that you make yourself. It is destined to become a family heirloom enjoyed by generations to come. Consider these ideas for simple, elegant ring pillows:

- Honor a beloved grandmother or great aunt by fashioning a ring pillow out of an heirloom handkerchief.
- If you're having your dress or your bridesmaids' dresses made, save a few swatches of material about 8 inches square for your ring pillow.
- Consider sewing on charms, colors, or symbols that reflect your ethnic heritage. For example, miniature horseshoes for Irish couples, blue fabric for Jewish couples, or phoenix and dragon imagery for Chinese couples.
- Use craft glue to affix small pressed flower petals to the material of your ring pillow.

TO MAKE A PILLOW:

2 pieces of 8-inch square fabric, sewing needle, thread, pillow stuffing, 10–12 inch satin ribbon, scissors

1. Pin together two pieces of 8 inch square fabric with the tops side faced together.

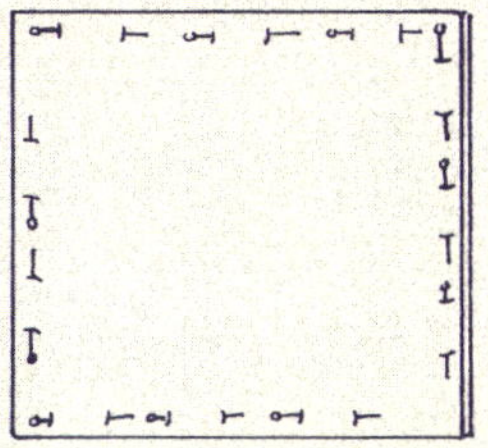

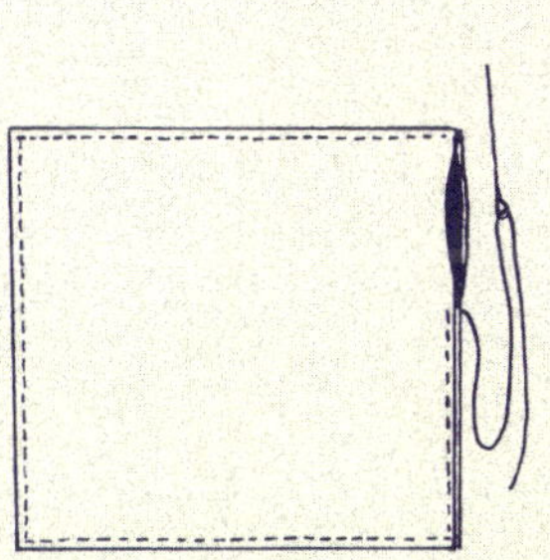

2. By hand or machine, sew a $\frac{1}{4}$-inch seam along the edges, leaving about two inches open on the last side.

3. Turn the pillow right side out and stuff with batting, feathers, or potpourri.

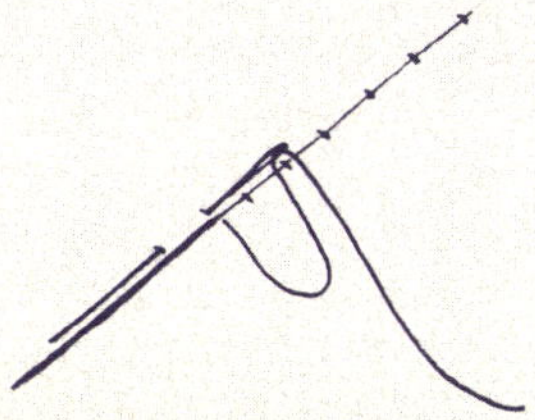

4. Sew the opening together by hand with a slipstitch.

5. Using needle and thread, attach the middle of a 10- to 12-inch satin ribbon to the center of the pillow with a small stitch.

6. Tie a knot with the loose ends of the ribbon. Rings can be tied on with an additional knot and bow.

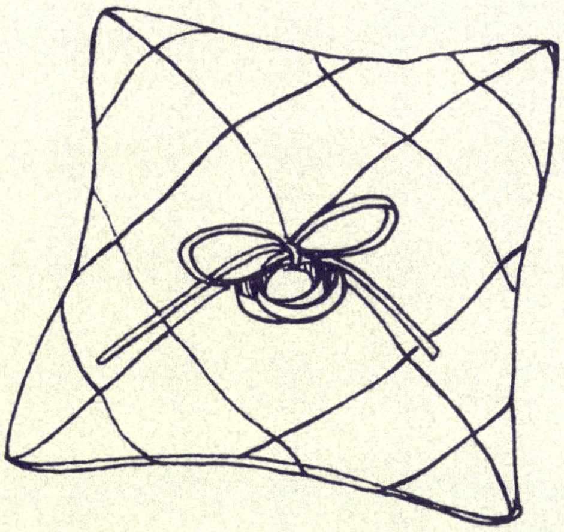

We have taken the seven steps. You have become mine forever. Yes, we have become partners. I have become yours. Hereafter, I cannot live without you. Do not live without me. Let us share the joys. We are word and meaning, united. You are thought and I am sound.

May the nights be honey-sweet for us; may the mornings be honey-sweet for us; may the earth be honey-sweet for us; may the heavens be honey-sweet for us.

May the plants be honey-sweet for us; may the sun be all honey for us; may the cows yield us honey-sweet milk!

As the heavens are stable, as the earth is stable, as the mountains are stable, as the whole universe is stable, so may our union be permanently settled.

FROM THE HINDU MARRIAGE RITUAL OF "SEVEN STEPS"

THE BOOK AND THE BROTHERHOOD

By Iris Murdoch

"...I HEREBY GIVE MYSELF. I love you. You are the only being whom I can love absolutely with my complete self, with all my flesh and mind and heart. You are my mate, my perfect partner, and I am yours. You must *feel* this now, as I do....It was a marvel that we ever met. It is some kind of divine luck that we are together now. We must never, never part again. We are, here in this, *necessary* beings, like gods. As we look at each other we verify, we *know*, the perfection of our love we *recognise* each other. *Here* is my life, here if need be is my death."

What will make your wedding unique? Perhaps a family custom that celebrates your cultural heritage. Or maybe a symbolic ritual to bless your marriage with children. Whether you borrow from the past or begin anew, you'll be continuing an age-old tradition of celebrating wishes of happiness, love, and fruitfulness in married life.

- IN KOREAN TRADITION, the groom presents his future mother-in-law with a goose, an animal which mates for life, to symbolize his fidelity to his new bride. The bride's mother shows her acceptance by offering noodles to the goose. Modern Korean grooms present wooden geese to their new in-laws, and the term "feeding noodles to the goose" remains a euphemism for getting married. Japanese couples will have a goose and gander join the wedding procession to bring good luck to their marriage.

Jumping the broom, feeding the goose.

AFRICAN-AMERICAN COUPLES celebrate the beginning of their new life together by jumping the broom, a custom practiced by Southern slaves, who were unable to marry legally. The ceremony, also known as a *besom* wedding, called for the groom to lay a broom on the ground with bristles facing north. He'd then take his bride's hand and they would jump over. The bride would then turn the broom around so that the bristles faced south, take her groom's hand, and they would jump over again. A similar custom of crossing sticks was practiced throughout Africa, Wales, and rural England. In addition to warding off bad luck, the broom or sticks alluded to the vitality of trees and symbolized the beginning of wedded life.

and tying the knot

- At the end of a Jewish ceremony, the groom crushes a glass under his foot as a remembrance of the fragility in life. The witnesses welcome the act with cheers of *Masel tov!* Some Japanese grooms will break an egg with their bare foot during the ceremony. The raw yoke symbolizes fertility.

- "Tying the knot" got started with the ancient Egyptians, and was also practiced by the medieval Celts. In a ceremony called handfasting, couples had their hands bound together while they pledged their fidelity. The practice is shared by Latin couples, who bind themselves together with cord, leather, or a vine. This custom survives in the Episcopal wedding ceremony, in which the minister binds the hands of the bride and groom together with his stole for part of the ceremony. In India, a marriage was considered legal and binding when the Hindu groom tied a ribbon around the neck of his bride. In ancient Carthage, a bride and groom were married by knotting their thumbs together with a leather strip. In ancient African custom, the groom would tie braided grasses around the bride's wrists and ankles.

❦ THE CUSTOM OF THROWING RICE has multiple origins. Once wedding guests would throw grains and figs at the newlyweds to wish them fertility. In Poland it was customary for onlookers to throw wheat and oats. After some noble weddings, the bride and groom would throw coins newly minted for the occasion. Modern wedding-goers throw birdseed, confetti, or flower petals, or blow bubbles over the newlyweds.

❦ IN A TRADITIONAL POLISH WEDDING, the *oczepiny*, or "capping ceremony," marks the moment when the bride becomes a married woman. The event takes place the evening of the wedding day, usually after the bride has danced with all the unmarried men. Young girls then remove the bride's wreath of rue, and married women place a cap on her head. Customarily, the bride removes the cap twice; the third time the women place it on her head, she keeps it on, joining in more singing and dancing.

Going!

Going!!

Gone!!!

Afoot and lighthearted, take to the
  open road,
Healthy, free, the world before you,
The long brown path before you
  leading wherever you choose.

Say only to one another:
Camerado, I give you my hand!
I give you my love more precious
  than money,
I give you myself before preaching or law:

Will you give me yourself? Will you
  come travel with me?
Shall we stick by each other as long
  as we live?

SONG OF THE OPEN ROAD
Walt Whitman

Often the traditional wedding banquet, symbolic of the official commencement of the new marriage, is as important as the ceremony itself. No matter what time of day the nuptials take place, many refer to the celebrated feast as the "bridal breakfast" because it is the first meal the bride and groom share as husband and wife. In some African communities, a couple is not considered married until the ceremonial breaking of bread. The word *bridal* comes from the term *bride's ale*, a common English festivity that would take place in a local tavern after the ceremony. Guests would pay for their own ale to help keep the wedding costs down.

Eat, drink, and be married!

The splendid array of food at Chinese and Japanese wedding banquets is rich with symbolism and good wishes for the couple's future. Each dish, through its color and presentation, evokes thoughts of abundance, love, fertility, and prosperity. Red foods, like lobster, tuna, and pork, are eaten for luck; noodles for long life; and chestnuts for many children. Vegetables make their appearance cut into fans for a bright future, cranes for fidelity, turtles for longevity. Many dishes blend cool and hot ingredients or sweet and sour flavors to represent the balance of yin and yang in marriage.

No feast is complete without the customary toasts to bless the bride and groom. This joyful tradition may have started among the wine lovers of France. At banquets, people customarily put a small bit of bread in a goblet to soak up the sediment from the wine. Guests would pass the goblet around for everyone to take a sip. The person who got the "toast" at the end would be rewarded with good luck.

CONFECTIONARY FAVORS

In the seventh century when weddings were regularly rowdy affairs, brides tacked favors of ribbons, flowers, and lace on their dresses. Immediately after the ceremony, guests ran to the bride and pulled them off for good luck, stripping the bride of all her adornments. Nowadays, favors can range from table centerpieces to little boxes of "groom's cake" for guests to take home. Edible favors are particularly popular among guests and couples alike. Personal and easy to make, fortune cookie favors are an original way to send your guests home with messages of love.

PERSONALIZED FORTUNE COOKIES

½ cup butter
1 cup confectioner's sugar
4 egg whites
½ teaspoon vanilla extract
1 cup pastry flour

1. Write lines from love poems or happy wishes on strips of paper about 4 inches long and ½ inch wide.
2. Preheat oven to 325°.
3. Make a simple French Tuile cookie dough by creaming ½ cup butter and 1 cup confectioner's suger together.
4. Beat in 4 egg whites and ½ teaspoon vanilla extract.
5. Mix in 1 cup pastry flour until just blended. Chill for 1 hour.
6. Spoon the batter onto a lined cookie sheet so that the dough spreads 5 to 6 inches in diameter during baking. Bake for 8 to 10 minutes and remove from oven.
7. While cookies are still warm and pliable, lay a fortune across the center of each. Gently fold the bottom half of each cookie up to meet the top half, then press your finger in the middle and bring the two ends together to form the fortune cookie.

Other suggested favors that can be either handcrafted or store-bought:

Take-Away Centerpieces

- A cluster of shallow dishes lined with attractive stones containing blooming paperwhites.
- A collection of small sand-filled decorative flowerpots holding elegant slender candles of various heights.

Place Card Keepsakes

- Mount decorative name placards onto poster board or foam matting, trim to size, then affix a magnet to the back of each one.

Gifts That Grow

- Wrap forget-me-not seed packets in ribbon or lace for guests to take home and plant in honor of the bride and groom.

The Gift of Music

- Create a CD containing a mix of many of the songs you plan to play during the wedding celebration.

For the Kids

- Goodie bags that hang on the back of each child's chair at the reception are sure to keep your young guests busy throughout your wedding day. Personalize simple canvas tote bags with iron-on letters spelling out each child's name. Fill the bags with colored pencils, a sketch book, activity books, jellybeans, candied almonds, a deck of playing cards, and stickers.

A day that is not danced

Where there's dancing, there's joy, especially at weddings. One of the most romantic moments is when the bride and groom dance together for the first time as a married couple, swaying and gliding to what is commonly known thereafter as "their song." Once the floor opens to everyone else, the festivities really begin, with the classic celebratory dances specially reserved for weddings. Here's a small sampling:

At Cajun weddings, unmarried girls traditionally **DANCE ALONE** with a broom. But in Slovakia, the bride dances with a broom to welcome a happy home life.

Bridesmaids and single women at a Norwegian wedding will blindfold the bride for the **"CROWN DANCE,"** for a chance to wear the bride's gold-and-silver-bangled headdress. Once the music begins, the bride tries to capture one of her single friends and crown her. The dancing continues until all the participants have had the opportunity to wear the crown.

Dancing is a central part of Irish weddings, where guests compete in contests to do **THE BEST JIG**. The winner takes the cake, literally: a miniature version of the wedding cake.

is a day that is not lived

One of the most festive moments at a Jewish wedding is the celebrated *Horah*, or **CHAIR DANCE**. Guests hoist up chairs holding the bride and groom and dance to "Hava Nagila." At Irish weddings, the groom's best lads will lift the groom up in a "jaunting chair" and dance him around the room.

The **MONEY DANCE** is a favorite in Poland, the Philippines, and Hawaii. Guests must pay to dance with the bride and groom by pinning money to their clothing or placing it in special pouches worn by the bride and groom.

A French Canadian custom allows the bride and groom to poke fun at their unmarried older siblings during **THE SOCK DANCE**. The single siblings wear colorful embroidered socks and take center stage while others tease them.

Italian brides and grooms dance **THE TARANTELLA**, an exotic dance that increases with speed as it nears the end, leaving everyone breathless and exhausted!

Some Favorite First Dance Songs

"A Fine Romance," Joe Derise

"Ain't No Mountain High Enough," Ashford & Simpson

"Ain't Nothing Like the Real Thing," Aretha Franklin

"And I Love Her," The Beatles

"Can't Take My Eyes Off You," Lauryn Hill

"Crazy for You," Madonna

"From This Moment On," Ella Fitzgerald

"Have I Told You Lately That I Love You," Van Morrison

"I Do," Paul Brandt

"I Love You," Martina McBride

"Is This Love," Bob Marley

"It Had to Be You," Harry Connick Jr.

"I Will Always Love You," Whitney Houston

"Love and Happiness," Al Green

"Love Me Tender," Elvis Presley

"My Cherie Amour," Stevie Wonder

"No Ordinary Love," Sade

"Someone Like You," Van Morrison

"Stand by My Woman," Lenny Kravitz

"Take My Breath Away," Berlin

"The First Time Ever I Saw Your Face," Roberta Flack

"What Is This Thing Called Love," Rosemary Clooney

"When a Man Loves a Woman," Percy Sledge

"When I Fall in Love," Nat King Cole

"Woman," John Lennon

"You Send Me," Aretha Franklin

You are my [husband/wife]
My feet shall run because of you.
My feet, dance because of you.
My heart shall beat because of you.
My eyes, see because of you.
My mind, think because of you.
And I shall love because of you.

ESKIMO LOVE SONG

Love does not consist in gazing at each other, but in looking outward together in the same direction.

ANTOINE DE SAINT-EXUPÉRY

Next to the bride and groom in all their finery, the wedding cake is often the grandest display of the nuptial celebration. For many purists, a proper wedding cake is an elaborately decorated work of culinary art no less than three tiers high. The top tier is often saved for a first anniversary or a christening.

A little slice of happiness

ONE OF THE MOST ANTICIPATED MOMENTS of the reception is the bride and groom's partaking of their first shared responsibility as a married couple: cutting the cake. The tradition started long before the invention of cake as we know it today. Ancient Greeks crumbled small biscuits on top of the bride's head in the belief that blessing her with a symbol of good fortune from the harvest would grant her ease in childbirth. The ancient Romans made bread-cakes from grain, salt, and water to break over the bride's head in a ceremony called *confarreatio*. Guests would scramble to catch the falling crumbs for good luck.

ALTHOUGH PEOPLE IN THE MIDDLE AGES missed out on the gastronomic pleasure of fine confectionery, they did much to inspire the modern wedding cake. Biscuits soon gave way to spicier breads and buns, which guests heaped in large piles at the wedding feast. The bride and groom then shared a kiss over the buns—the kiss was said to bless them with good luck—before distributing the pastries to their guests. Bakers caught on to this custom and started icing the buns with honey to make them stick together and therefore stack more easily. These festive treats were the precursors to the modern-day "groom's cake," traditionally kept in small boxes for the guests to take home.

BY THE SIXTEENTH CENTURY, spiced plum cakes were all the rage at weddings. These dense, heavy breads were filled with dried raisins, currants, plums, and in some cases almonds. For centuries, these alcohol-preserved concoctions remained the most common style of wedding cake. It wasn't until the 1800s that the French discovered the secrets of baking powder and baking soda and developed the fine milled flours used today. *Voilà!* The contemporary wedding cake was born.

THANKS TO QUEEN VICTORIA and other royals, the craze for elaborate, multi-tiered cakes spread throughout Europe. The primary centerpiece of Queen Victoria's wedding was a plum cake that measured 3 yards in circumference and 14 inches in depth, and weighed 300 pounds! In 1923, the Viscount Lascelles and Princess Mary topped that with a royal wedding cake that stood 9 feet tall and weighed a whopping 800 pounds.

GROOM'S CAKE

In the Southern United States, the groom's cake started as a second layer of dark wedding cake on top of a larger layer of white cake. The bridal couple would cut cake from the bottom tier, and serve the dark cake on a later date. By the late 1800s, the groom's cake became a separate dessert to be divided and presented to guests in small white boxes.

In the American tradition, groom's cakes are often rich chocolate cakes, although they may be fruit or nut cakes as well. In some cases the groom's cake reflects the groom's personality; instead of being served in boxes, it will be a large sheet cake in the shape of a sailboat or football, for example. For an elegant twist on the tradition, make a tiered tower of chocolate cupcakes that can be taken home by guests as wedding favors at the end of the reception. The recipe that follows includes a sprinkling of ground almonds, an ingredient that symbolizes undying love. Each batch makes 12 cupcakes. Repeat the recipe until the number of cupcakes equals the number of guests.

CHOCOLATE CUPCAKE TOWER

4 tablespoons cocoa powder (preferably Dutch)

1/2 cup boiling water

3/4 cup sugar

1 1/2 cup self-rising cake flour

3/4 cup very soft unsalted butter

2 large eggs

1 teaspoon vanilla extract

12-cup muffin pan lined with paper baking cups

1. Preheat the oven to 400°. In a stainless steel bowl, mix the cocoa to a paste with the boiling water and set aside to cool.

2. Mix the sugar and the flour. In a large bowl add the butter and 1/2 of the cocoa mixture. Mix well and put aside.

3. Beat the eggs, the rest of the cocoa mixture and the vanilla well. Dribble slowly into the sugar mixture, beating constantly until it is creamy.

4. Spoon into the paper baking cups in the pan and bake for 20 minutes, until a toothpick comes out clean.

5. Leave in the pan for 5 minutes, then remove the cupcakes in the paper baking cups and cool on a wire rack. Cool completely before frosting.

FROSTING & DECORATION

1 1/3 cups confectioner's sugar, sifted

4 ounces cream cheese

3 oz. bittersweet chocolate shavings

3 oz. ground almonds

1. When the cupcakes are completely cool, make the frosting by beating together the sifted confectioner's sugar and cream cheese until soft.

2. Frost cupcakes and sprinkle with ground almonds and chocolate shavings.

3. Stack cupcakes in square layers, making a tiered tower. The size of the base layer will depend on the total number of cupcakes being used. Each ascending layer should be one less cupcake in width. For example, to make a 140-cupcake tower, here's how to stack each layer:

1st layer:	7 cupcakes wide (49 cupcakes)
2nd layer:	6 cupcakes wide (36 cupcakes)
3rd layer:	5 cupcakes wide (25 cupcakes),
4th layer:	4 cupcakes wide (16 cupcakes)
5th layer:	3 cupcakes wide (9 cupcakes)
6th layer:	2 cupcakes wide (4 cupcakes)
7th layer:	1 cupcake

Success in marriage depends on being able, when you get over being in love, to really love.... You never know anyone until you marry them.

ELEANOR ROOSEVELT

WUTHERING HEIGHTS

By Emily Brontë

In this excerpt from Emily Brontë's classic novel, Catherine explains the depth of her love for Heathcliff, the man she truly loves but did not marry.

...HE'S MORE MYSELF THAN I AM. Whatever our souls are made of, his and mine are the same....If all else perished and *he* remained, and he were annihilated, the universe would turn to a might stranger....He's always, always in my mind; not as a pleasure to myself, but as my own being.

The great secret of a successful marriage is to treat all disasters as incidents and none of the incidents as disasters.

SIR HAROLD NICOLSON

Wedding celebrations are often rife with frolicsome antics and pranksters who revel at playing tricks on the bride and groom. Many of these good-humored festivities originated from old superstitions about keeping evil spirits away or protecting the bride from thieving marauders. In any event, the fun and games allow others to wish happiness and prosperity to the newlyweds and, in some cases, garner good luck for themselves!

Merriment & mischief

IT'S CONSIDERED GOOD LUCK AT IRISH WEDDINGS when the Straw Boys arrive. The custom prevailed in the countryside, where uninvited young men, with straw stuffed in their hats and clothes to disguise their appearance, would gate-crash wedding parties, often providing music and dance entertainment. In the midst of their singing and merriment, they usually insisted upon dancing with the bride until offered food and drink. At the end of the night, the bride and groom were crowned with smaller straw hats. A symbol of fertility, straw was thought to bring good luck to the couple.

Standes-
Amt.

IN THE SIXTEENTH AND SEVENTEENTH CENTURIES, when most weddings were raucous affairs, guests regularly chased the bride and groom to their honeymoon chambers and invaded their room. Just about everything concerning the bride and groom was considered good luck—including their clothing. The bride would relent, throwing a stocking at the single women, who clamored to catch it and be next to wed. Today, the stocking has been replaced with a garter worn around the bride's leg.

IN THE RURAL UNITED STATES, newlyweds can expect a late-night "shivaree" from noisy friends and neighbors. The crowd serenades the couple with boisterous shouting until the husband humors them with treats. The practice is also called "belling," "collathump," and "skimmilton." In some cases the group might continue their revelry in the couple's new home, taking all the labels off the canned goods or forcing the bride and groom to do stunts. The custom comes from the medieval French *chariviari*, which means a loud display of rough music.

THE GERMAN CUSTOM OF STEALING THE BRIDE has its roots in medieval abductions. During the reception the groom's best man whisks the bride away to a bar, where they drink champagne until the groom finds them and pays their tab. In Wales, the bride and her family ride away on horseback, with members of the groom's family and his groomsmen in pursuit. Sometimes the custom ends in a raucous mock battle wherein the groomsmen "fetch the bride" for the ceremony.

GERMAN COUPLES have a lively night of feasting and frolicking on *Polterabend*. The night before the wedding, friends, neighbors, and unexpected visitors descend upon the couple for a rowdy evening. As part of the festivities, guests put on a mock play of what the bride and groom's married life will be like, and they might string baby items on the clothesline. After a night of dancing and drinking, guests will break the old china and crystal to symbolize a fresh start for the new couple. The bride and groom sweep up the shards to assure their good fortune in a happy home with many children.

Never above you.
Never below you.
Always beside you.

WALTER WINCHELL

That romantic moment when the groom carries his bride over the threshold isn't just a display of gallantry; it's an ancient homage to the protector of hearth and home. The virgin Roman goddess Vespa considered the threshold sacred. Ancient Roman grooms therefore carried out this symbolic gesture to avoid letting their virgin brides touch the threshold and thereby risk being disrespectful of the goddess.

Home is where the heart is

IN SOUTH AFRICA, to symbolize the fire of a new family's hearth, both sets of parents bring fire from their own homes to light the first fire in the bride and groom's new home.

THE CHIMNEY was a traditional passageway for unwanted spirits to enter the home. Upon their initial entry, Russian couples burn straw in the hearth to smoke out any demons that might be hiding in the flue.

Other cultures feared that evil spirits lurked in the ground near the threshold, waiting to trip the bride as she entered. Some brides would toss grains of salt across the threshold to ward off malevolent spirits. The belief was that if a witch were to try and enter the newlywed's home, she would have to stop and count every grain of salt before she could come inside, and would get discouraged and leave.

Many couples christen their new homes with symbols of fidelity and fertility. French brides break an egg in the doorway to ensure healthy and happy children. Spanish brides are known to keep an olive branch in the house to make sure their husbands stay faithful. In Greece, the bride's mother meets the bride at the door of the newlyweds' home. The mother gives the new bride a drink of honey and water so that her words will always be sweet. She then uses the rest of the drink to paint the threshold, so that their home remains a place of sweetness and peace.

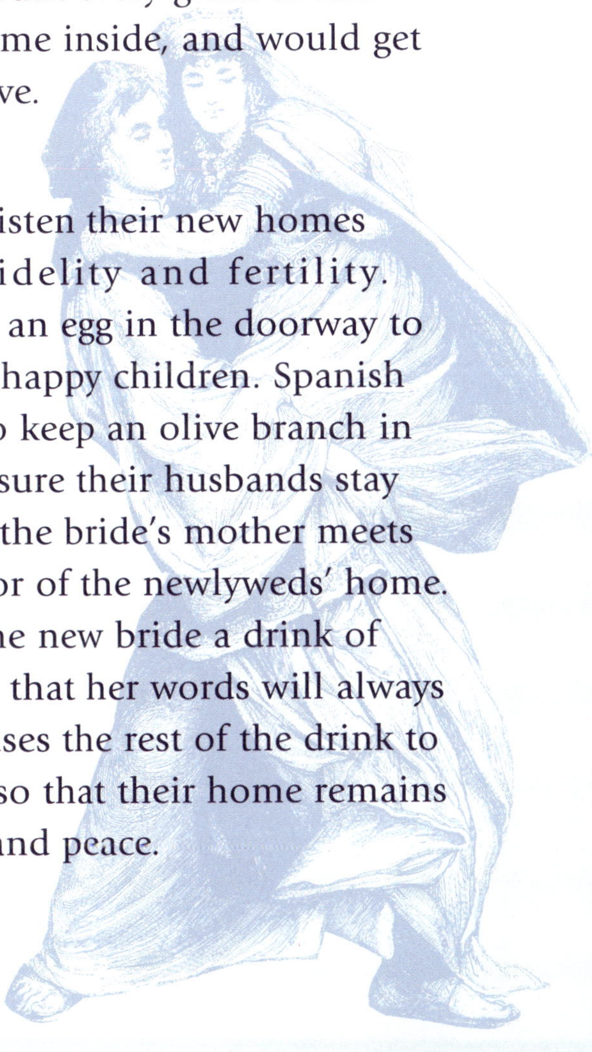

FENG SHUI YOUR MARRIAGE

FENG SHUI IS AN ANCIENT SYSTEM that strives to achieve harmony between people and their environment. Based on the Taoist tradition of perceiving nature as five elemental energies (*chi*), Feng Shui masters try to understand the natural order of cause and effect: why things happen to us when they do, and by extension, what we can do to steer ourselves onto a different path. Reordering *chi* in your environment can affect every aspect of your life—even your chances of a happy marriage. Here are a few tips to encourage good *chi* on your wedding day and in the marital home.

FENG SHUI YOUR WEDDING

- A bride should go to her wedding in a red car, but if that isn't possible, either a maroon, yellow, or white vehicle makes a good substitute for enhancing strong *yang* energy. An endless knot should also be tied to the front of the car, which signifies undying love between the couple.
- When the bride and groom arrive at the reception venue, they should be greeted by a loud sound, such as the band playing a rousing rendition of the wedding march—this has the double effect of representing *yang* energies while also announcing the start of the celebration.

- When decorating the reception hall, make sure that there are no dried flowers anywhere, including potpourri. It's also a good idea to have all the colors of the nine lives represented somewhere within the hall—dark blue or black, red, yellow, pink, gold or purple, gray or silver, and white. This will help keep all the energies balanced, giving the couple an auspicious beginning to their marriage.

- The wedding vows should be exchanged within red envelopes. The red color symbolizes strong *yang* energy, which will imbue your words with power and luck, while the rectangular shape of the envelope heralds back to the protection provided by ancient Chinese shields.

- Newlyweds should follow the ancient Chinese tradition of drinking tea with their parents right after the wedding when they are still in their wedding clothes, so that they may honor their elders and receive their blessings.

FENG SHUI YOUR HOME

- Before a newlywed couple moves in together, the following feng shui ritual should be performed to bring good fortune to all eight corners of their house. Mix a dash of saffron with water until it yellows, and pour a few drops on every floor in the northern end of the home, known as the water sector, to help kindle and sustain love. In the northeast and southwest areas, fill a bucket with sand from a riverbank and mix it with the ashes from three incense sticks. Scatter the sand over the corners, and wait a day before cleaning it up to activate energy in the two earth sectors of your home. In the east and southeast, the two wood areas, place seven flowers—lily, peony, chrysanthemum, plum blossom, lotus blossom, orchid, and a bulb flower. If any of these are unavailable, choose blooms from each of the four seasons to bring good fortune all year-round. In the southern fire sector, activate *yang* energy by lighting three red candles. In the west and northwest metal sectors, strengthen the *chi* with three gold or silver pieces. Walk around this sector with a dish of these in hand.

- It is bad feng shui to have the marital bed reflected in a mirror. In fact, the larger a mirror is, the more negative chi a marriage will have, because mirrors can leave couples wanting to look elsewhere for more satisfaction. While positioning mirrors directly behind the bed or covering them with a heavy drape can lessen the potential harm, it's best to remove them entirely from the bedroom.

- Light earth tones are the perfect color for your bedroom because earth energies nurture your body. Fiery colors like red and hot orange should be avoided. While they do incite the passions, they also keep you from a restful sleep. Colors like blue and purple should be kept away from the bed at all costs since they have a servile and chaste connotation.

- It is important to remove anything with pointy corners from your bedroom, such as your dresser, especially if it's at head-level. This sends out negative energy, or *shar* chi, and can cause stress and disputes between couples. Ideally, your furniture should be round and curved, which gives off good *chi* by mimicking the form of the human body.

- To promote a good relationship, try to double up when you decorate. For instance, instead of one bedside lamp, consider a pair, one for each side of the bed. Two pieces of rose quartz are particularly auspicious in the bedroom. While the mandarin duck is thought to bring good fortune to those who have not yet found a mate, a pair of flying geese symbolizes the happiness of marriage, and helps to reinforce the fidelity of a couple.

The last bit of cake has been eaten, the last dance done, the last farewell spoken—and at last the bride and groom are alone to let the honeymoon begin.... Not necessarily!

In the sixteenth century, the groomsmen and bridesmaids saw to the bedding of the bride and groom. The attendants first blessed the nuptial bed by lacing it with ribbons and surrounding it with fragrant herbs before shepherding the newlyweds to their bridal chamber. They then undressed the couple and placed them in bed. Often, the attendants served the bride and groom "sack-posset," a spiced hot milk fermented with wine or ale. Pranksters might sew the sheets together or tie bells to the newlyweds' bedsprings.

In the Irish countryside, friends of the bridal couple bless the nuptial bed by fetching an egg-laying hen and tying it to the bedposts in hopes of procuring a fresh egg on the bride-bed. It was also hoped that some of the hen's fertility would be passed on to the couple.

The first night

IN AFRICA AND CHINA, friends of the wedding pair place a baby or fresh fruit in the bed before the bride and groom share it. After a Chinese wedding banquet, many of the guests warm up the bridal bed and cajole the newlyweds into playing erotic games, such as giving the groom wine that he must transfer to the bride's mouth or scattering beans on the bride's body for the groom to pick up with his mouth.

IN ANCIENT TIMES, fire played an important role on the honeymoon night. The Roman bride was escorted to the bridal chamber by torchlight and the torch was later thrown to the wedding guests. According to early Polish custom, a new bride's bedchamber was laden with flowers, and male guests would circle the room with burning candles to chase away demons before the groom could enter.

IT WAS CUSTOMARY in the late eighteenth and early nineteenth centuries for Irish newlyweds to take a different path home from their wedding festivities than the one they took to the wedding. This was to avoid the pranks of friends and family as well as the *sidhe*, or faeries, who were thought to be waiting to whisk the bride away and steal her fine dress.

of the rest of your life

SUPERSTITION DICTATES in many parts of the world that if the bride and groom sleep with their heads facing north (the compass point of happiness) on their wedding night, they will have happiness in their married life.

Believe it or not, the following is an excerpt from the Madison Institute Newsletter, Fall 1894:

INSTRUCTION AND ADVICE FOR THE YOUNG BRIDE

BY RUTH SMYTHERS, BELOVED WIFE OF THE REVEREND L.D. SMYTHERS

To the sensitive young woman who has had the benefits of proper upbringing, the wedding day is, ironically, both the happiest and the most terrifying day of her life. On the positive side, there is the wedding itself, in which the bride is the central attraction in a beautiful and inspiring ceremony, symbolising her triumph in securing a male to provide for all her needs for the rest of her life. On the negative side, there is the wedding night, during which the bride must pay the piper, so to speak, by facing for the first time the terrible experience of sex.

At this point, dear reader, let me concede one shocking truth. Some young women actually anticipate the wedding night ordeal with curiosity and pleasure! Beware such an attitude! A selfish and sensual husband can easily take advantage of such a bride. One cardinal rule of marriage should never be forgotten: GIVE LITTLE, GIVE SELDOM, AND ABOVE ALL, GIVE GRUDGINGLY. Otherwise, what could have been a proper marriage could become an orgy of sexual lust.

On the other hand, the bride's terror need not be extreme. While sex is at best revolting and at worst rather painful, it has to be endured, and has been by women since the beginning of time, and is compensated for by the monogamous home and by the children produced through it. It is useless, in most cases, for the bride to prevail upon the groom to forgo the sexual initiation. While the ideal husband would be one who would approach his bride only at her request, and only for the purpose of begetting offspring, such nobility and unselfishness cannot be expected from the average man.

Most men, if not denied, would demand sex almost every day. The wise bride will permit a maximum of two brief sexual experiences weekly during the first months of the marriage. As time goes by she should make every effort to reduce this frequency.

Feigned illness, sleepiness, and headaches are among the wife's best friends in this matter. Arguments, nagging, scolding and bickering also prove very effective, if used in the late evening about an hour before the husband would normally commence his seduction.

Clever wives are ever on the alert for new and better methods of denying and discouraging the amorous overtures of the husband. A good wife should expect to have reduced sexual contacts to once a week by the end of the first year of marriage and to once a month by the end of the fifth year of marriage.

Just as she should be ever alert to keep the quantity of sex as low as possible, the wise bride will pay equal attention to limiting the kind and degree of sexual contacts. Most men are by nature rather perverted, and if given half a chance, would engage in quite a variety of the most revolting practices. These practices include amongst others performing the normal act in abnormal positions.

When he finds her, the wife should lie as still as possible. Bodily motion on her part could be interpreted as sexual excitement by the optimistic husband. If he attempts to kiss her on the lips she should turn her head slightly so that the kiss falls harmlessly on her cheek instead. If he attempts to kiss her hand, she should make a fist. If he lifts her gown and attempts to kiss her anyplace else, she should quickly pull the gown back in place, spring from the bed and announce that nature calls her to the toilet. This will generally dampen his desire to kiss in the forbidden territory.

If the husband attempts to seduce her with lascivious talk, the wise wife will suddenly remember some trivial non-sexual question to ask him. Once he answers she should keep the conversation going no matter how frivolous it may seem at the time. Eventually the husband will learn that if he insists on having sexual contact, he must get on with it without amorous embellishment.

As soon as the husband has completed the act, the wise wife will start nagging him about various minor tasks she wishes him to perform on the morrow. Many men obtain a major portion of their sexual satisfaction from the peaceful exhaustion immediately after the act is over. Thus the wife must insure that there is no peace in this period for him to enjoy. Otherwise, he might be encouraged to soon try for more.

One heartening factor for which the wife can be grateful is the fact that the husband's home, school, church, and social environment have been working together all through his life to instill in him a deep sense of guilt in regards to his sexual feelings, so that he comes to the marriage couch apologetically and filled with shame, already half cowed and subdued. The wise wife seizes upon this advantage and relentlessly pursues her goal first to limit, later to annihilate completely, her husband's desire for sexual expression.

Chains do not hold a marriage together. It is threads, hundreds of tiny threads which sew people together through the years. That is what makes a marriage last.

SIMONE SIGNORET

After all the hectic preparations for the Big Day, many couples today opt for a few peaceful, relaxing weeks in sunny seclusion. But honeymoons haven't always been languorous and restful.

A month of wine and honey

THE EARLIEST HONEYMOONS were not necessarily periods of happy celebration for newlyweds, but rather forced seclusion for the bride. In the days when marriage by abduction was not yet outlawed, a groom would capture a bride from a village or rival tribe and take her into seclusion until tempers had cooled or the tribe had moved on. The groom would often return alone to negotiate a bride-price with her father to prevent an outbreak of fighting. The kidnapped bride would be held captive and sedated with honey wine for a full cycle of the moon, after which time the couple was considered married. Out of this tradition, eloping couples that ran off together and drank honey wine for a month, "until the moon waned," were considered married.

THE IRISH translation for honeymoon is *mi na meala*, which means the "month of honey." This stems from the ancient Germanic tribal custom of the newlyweds' drinking mead laced with honey—in preparation for the bitter and the sweet of marriage—every day for a full cycle of the moon. This month of honey became known as the honeymoon.

IN JAPAN, it was customary for the groom to prepare for the honeymoon by overseeing the installation of the bridal bed the day before the wedding. A "good luck woman" or a "good luck man"—that is, a man or woman with many children and a living mate was selected to "install" the newly purchased bed. After the bed was in place, children were invited onto the bed as an omen of fertility. The bed was scattered with red dates, oranges, lotus seeds, peanuts, pomengranates, and other fruits for the same reason.

Top 5 Honeymoon Locations

HAWAII With its perfect weather, volcanoes, valleys, waterfalls, nightlife, and black sand beaches, Hawaii is the ideal honeymoon destination for newlyweds.

WALT DISNEY WORLD Get ready to be a kid again. Any one of the great honeymoon packages offers deluxe accommodations at a select Disney resort and unlimited passes to any of the fun-filled theme parks.

ITALY Take a gondola ride in Venice. Bask in the Renaissance beauty of Florence. Rent a villa on Lake Como. No matter what your destination is, Italy will not disappoint.

NIAGARA FALLS A long-time traditional location for honeymoons. Newlyweds can ride a boat under the majestic falls in the Maid of the Mist.

PARIS, FRANCE It's not called the most romantic city for nothing! Stroll along the Seine, take in a museum, or have a romantic dinner at one of the hundreds of brasseries. Paris really is for lovers!

IN BULGARIA the bride and groom disappear for a week to spend their first days as husband and wife in seclusion. The bride then makes a visit to the village well, accompanied by a group of married women. She circles the well three times and kisses the hands of all of the women who have come with her. The women then present her with figs to wish her a fruitful and happy life.

Better to have loved a short man than never to have loved a tall.

DAVID CHAMBLESS

Love is enough: though the World be a-waning,
And the woods have no voice but the voice of complaining,
Though the sky be too dark for dim eyes to discover
The gold-cups and daisies fair blooming thereunder,
Though the hills be held shadows, and the sea a dark wonder
And this day draw a veil over all deeds passed over,
Yet their hands shall not tremble, their feet shall not falter;
The void shall not weary, the fear shall not alter
These lips and these eyes of the loved and the lover.

LOVE IS ENOUGH
William Morris

NEWLYWED DINNER

The wedding may be over, but your life as a married couple is just beginning. Keep the passion of your honeymoon alive with an aphrodisiac dinner for two to celebrate your first month (or week!) together. Throughout history, certain foods have been believed to stimulate the libido because of their suggestive shapes, texture, or nutritional content. Second-century Roman satirist Juvenal was the first to note the amorous nature of women after consuming large quantities of wine and "giant oysters," which not only resemble female genitalia, but are also very rich in protein. Another powerful sexual stimulant is chocolate, which the Aztecs relished as the "nourishment of the gods." In the towns of France, eating strawberries is still considered to be an extremely potent way for newlyweds to nourish their libido.

Create the mood for romance by setting a romantic candlelit table for two. Then stir up some passion with this aphrodisiac-laden menu:

Appetizer

CHAMPAGNE OYSTERS WITH POTATO CAKES

POTATO CAKES

2 large potatoes, cleaned, peeled, and grated

½ large onion, finely chopped

1 tablespoon fresh lemon juice

1 large egg, lightly beaten

1 tablespoon chopped fresh parsley

Salt and freshly ground pepper to taste

2 tablespoons vegetable oil

1. Preheat the oven to 200° F. Place a baking sheet on middle rack of oven.
2. In a medium-sized bowl combine the grated potatoes and chopped onions. Add the lemon juice and toss.
3. Place the potato and onion mixture in a clean kitchen towel and squeeze dry. Transfer to a small bowl and add the egg and parsley. Mix well. Season with salt and pepper.
4. Using the palms of your hands, form mixture into 2 patties.
5. Heat vegetable oil in a large skillet, over medium heat. Add the potato cakes to the skillet, pressing down on each patty until flat and even all the way around. Sauté the potato cakes until golden brown (about 3 minutes for each side.)
6. Transfer to baking sheet in the oven to keep warm while you are preparing the oysters.

CHAMPAGNE OYSTERS

½ cup champagne
1 ½ tablespoons finely chopped shallots
¾ cup heavy cream
4 tablespoons unsalted butter, softened
12 oysters, freshly shucked
1 tablespoon fresh thyme
1 teaspoon chives
Salt and pepper to taste

1. In a medium saucepan, combine the champagne and shallots over medium heat. Simmer until the liquid is reduced by half.
2. Slowly add the cream, whisking constantly. Return to a simmer until liquid is reduced by one quarter. Slowly add the butter, a tablespoon at a time, whisking until thickened.
3. Add the oysters to the sauce and simmer gently until the oysters are firm. Add thyme, and season with salt and pepper.
4. To serve, place potato patties on prewarmed plates and spoon 6 oysters onto each cake. Drizzle sauce over the oysters, top with caviar (optional), and sprinkle with chives. Serve immediately.

Serves 2

Entrée

LOBSTER & LINGUINE WITH TOMATO-BASIL SAUCE

2 small live lobsters (1 to 1 1/4 lbs each)

1 tablespoon extra-virgin olive oil

1 tablespoon chopped garlic

3 cups chopped fresh vine-ripened tomatoes or 1 14-ounce can tomatoes (with juices)

1/4 cup dry white wine

1/2 cup slivered basil leaves

1/4 cup light cream

salt and freshly ground black pepper

1 lb. fresh linguine

1. In a large pot, bring 2 inches water to a boil. Put lobsters in headfirst, cover tightly and steam until the lobsters are bright red, 10 to 12 minutes. Remove and let cool slightly. Separate tails from bodies, twist off claws, remove all the meat and cut into large chunks; discard shells.
2. In a large deep skillet, heat oil over medium-high heat. Add garlic and sauté until the garlic is tender, about 2 minutes. Stir in tomatoes and wine and bring to a simmer. Add 1/4 cup of the basil and continue to simmer until the sauce has thickened slightly (about 2 minutes). Add salt and pepper to taste.
3. Remove the skillet from the heat, add cream and toss to combine. Add the reserved lobster meat to the sauce.
4. Meanwhile, cook linguine in a large pot of boiling salted water until al dente (2 to 3 minutes). Drain the linguine and toss with the sauce. Garnish with the remaining basil and serve.

Serves 2

Dessert

CHOCOLATE-DIPPED STRAWBERRIES

½ pint fresh strawberries, stems intact

4 ounces bittersweet chocolate, broken into chunks

½ tablespoon solid white vegetable shortening

½ cup of white chocolate chips

1. Rinse strawberries thoroughly under running water, pat with paper towels, and leave to air-dry.
2. Pour about 1 inch of water into bottom of a double boiler and heat over low heat until hot but not simmering. Melt the milk chocolate and shortening together in the top of double boiler, stirring occasionally until smooth.
3. Working quickly, swirl each strawberry gently in the chocolate about halfway up the fruit and place on a piece of wax paper to cool and harden. When cool, place in refrigerator to further set chocolate shell, about a half hour.
4. Meanwhile, clean and replace the top of your double boiler, and use to melt white chocolate chips, stirring until smooth over low heat.
5. Place cooled strawberries on serving dish and drizzle with melted white chocolate. Refrigerate until you are ready to serve. They go perfectly with a chilled glass of champagne.

Serves 2 (with some left over for a midnight snack!)

A good marriage is that in which each

RAINER MARIA RILKE

appoints the other guardian of his solitude.

Marriage is one long conversation, chequered by disputes... But in the intervals, almost unconsciously, and with no desire to shine, the whole material of life is turned over and over ideas are struck out and shared, the two persons more and more adapt their notions one to suit the other, and in process of time, without sound of trumpet, they conduct each other into new worlds of thought.

ROBERT LOUIS STEVENSON (1850 – 1894)

It's never too soon to start looking ahead! Every year, when the calendar falls on the anniversary of their wedding, married couples rekindle the romance and memories of their most important day.

Grow old along with me,
the best is yet to be

Husbands and wives often spend their first anniversary alone together, while later anniversaries tend to be big celebratory bashes. In England, couples enjoying their diamond anniversary receive a special telegram from the queen. The custom of saving the top layer of the wedding cake to share on the first anniversary predates the icebox. In those days, cakes were made of dried fruit, alcohol, and marzipan, and could easily keep for a year or longer.

Anniversary Gifts

	TRADITIONAL	CONTEMPORARY
YEAR 1:	PAPER	CLOCKS
YEAR 2:	COTTON	CHINA
YEAR 3:	LEATHER	CRYSTAL, GLASS
YEAR 4:	LINEN	ELECTRICAL APPLIANCES
YEAR 5:	WOOD	SILVERWARE
YEAR 6:	IRON	WOOD
YEAR 7:	WOOL, COPPER, BRASS	DESK SETS
YEAR 8:	BRONZE	LINEN, LACE
YEAR 9:	POTTERY, WILLOW	LEATHER
YEAR 10:	TIN, ALUMINUM	DIAMOND JEWELRY
YEAR 11:	STEEL	FASHION JEWELRY
YEAR 12:	SILK	PEARLS
YEAR 13:	LACE	TEXTILES, FUR
YEAR 14:	IVORY	GOLD JEWELRY
YEAR 15:	CRYSTAL	WATCHES
YEAR 20:	CHINA	PLATINUM
YEAR 25:	SILVER	STERLING SILVER
YEAR 30:	PEARLS	DIAMONDS
YEAR 35:	CORAL	JADE
YEAR 40:	RUBIES	GARNETS
YEAR 45:	SAPPHIRES	TOURMALINES
YEAR 50:	GOLD	GOLD

We two form a multitude.

OVID

SOWING THE SEEDS OF LOVE

THE CUSTOM OF PLANTING a flower bush or tree as a symbol of stability, growth, and fertility has long played a part in marriages and weddings. In many places around the world, newlyweds still celebrate their union with this ritual. In the village of Lucerne, Switzerland, couples plant pine trees to promote happiness and fertility. This dates back to an ancient tradition in which the groom proposed to his beloved by planting trees in her yard embellished with large decorative ribbons. In Holland, the houses of the newly married can be distinguished by the presence of freshly turned soil and newly planted lilies-of-the-valley. It is thought that these flowers represent a "return of happiness" that is renewed with their blooming every spring. The following planting instructions are for the bridal wreath spirea, a popular, beautiful, and aptly named shrub to use for this romantic tradition.

PLANTING A BRIDAL WREATH

- The bridal wreath spirea is one of the least finicky flowering shrubs out there, and can prove to be quite hardy. Before planting the bridal bush, clear a spot in the garden of any sod or weeds. Make sure that it is an open space with lots of sunlight—bridal wreaths grow very quickly, and after many years can reach a maximum width of 20 feet and a height of 6 to 10 feet.

- It is a good idea to keep the roots together with the soil they came in. Never let the roots come in contact with fresh manure or any other kind of fertilizer.

- Spread the roots evenly around in the hole, and make sure that the soil is packed carefully to cover the roots without any air pockets.

- To prevent too much water drainage, pack the soil around the top so that it forms a dish around the bush.

- Once the soil has been packed, give the bush a heavy watering. Don't worry about giving it too much water. Afterward, place a layer of mulch around the bush. Rotted bark, sawdust, or leaf mold will all help keep the soil moist.

- Be generous with water during the first season, but not to the point where the soil becomes soggy.

**Understand, I'll slip quietly
away from the noisy crowd
when I see the pale
stars rising, blooming, over the oaks.**

**I'll pursue solitary pathways
through the pale twilit meadows,
with only this one dream:
You come too.**

Rainer Maria Rilke

Never go to bed angry.
Stay up and fight.

PHYLLIS DILLER